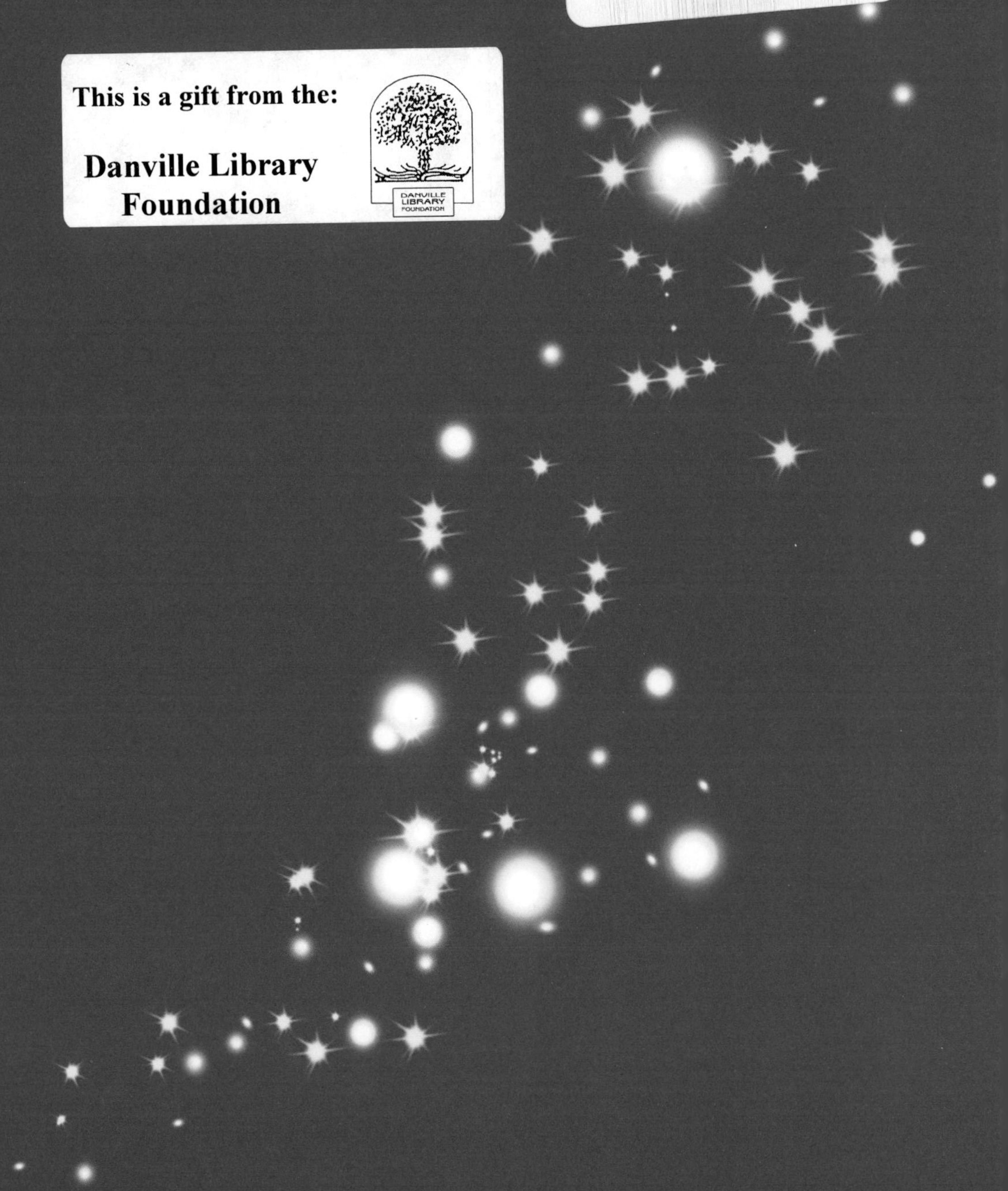

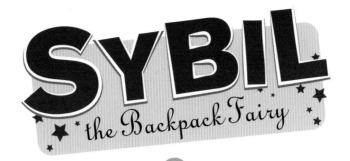

SYBIL the Backpack Fairy

3

"AITHOR"

MICHEL RODRIGUE • Writer
ANTONELLO DALENA & MANUELA RAZZI • Artists
CECILIA GIUMENTO • Colorist

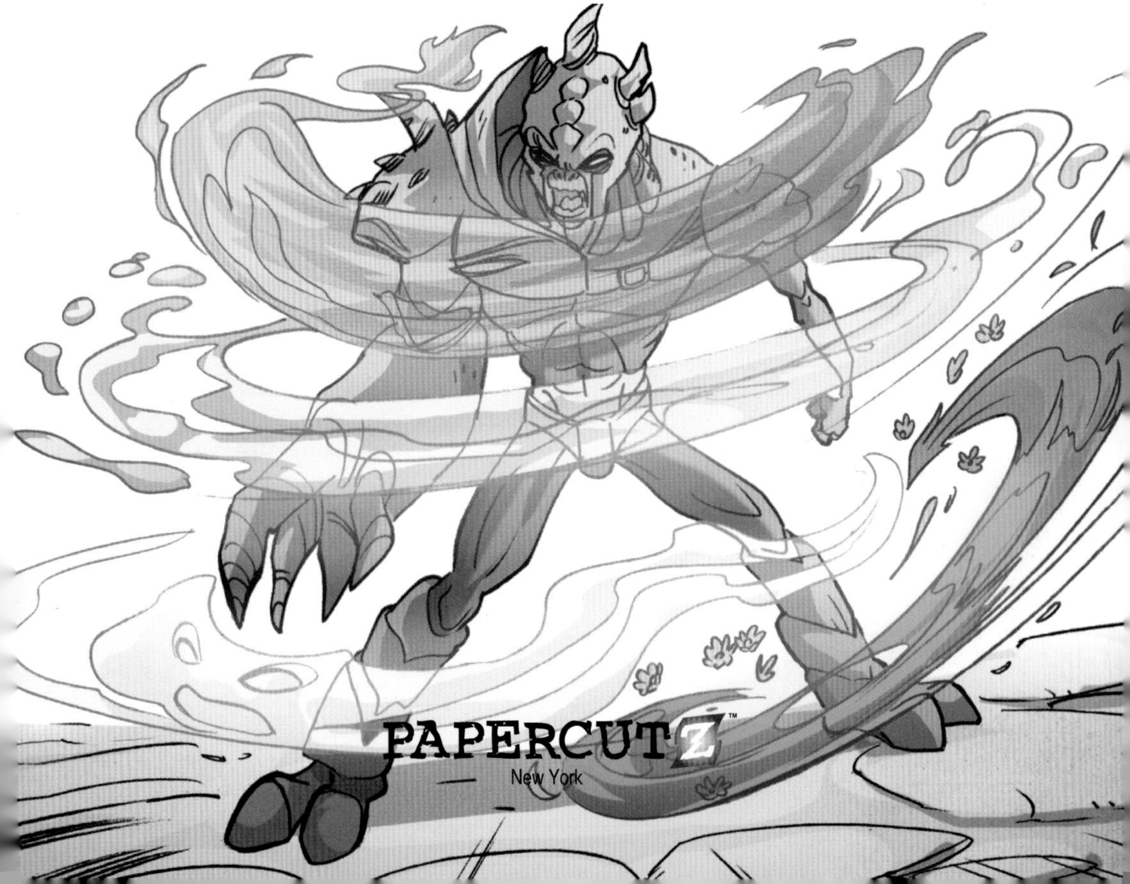

PAPERCUTZ™
New York

SYBIL
the Backpack Fairy

GRAPHIC NOVELS
AVAILABLE FROM

PAPERCUTZ™

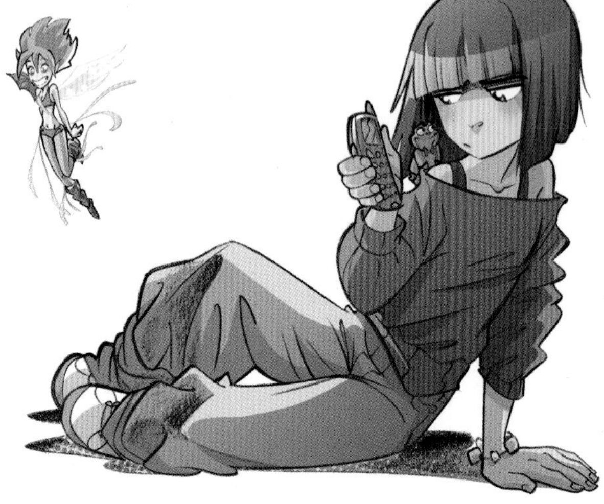

COMING SOON!

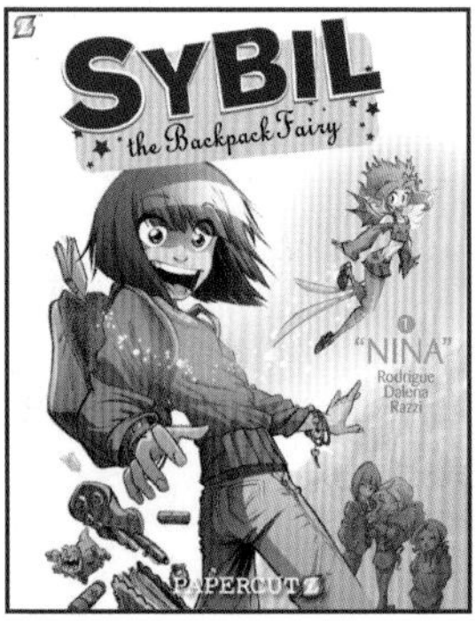
SYBIL
the Backpack Fairy
1 "NINA"
Rodrigue
Dalena
Razzi
PAPERCUTZ

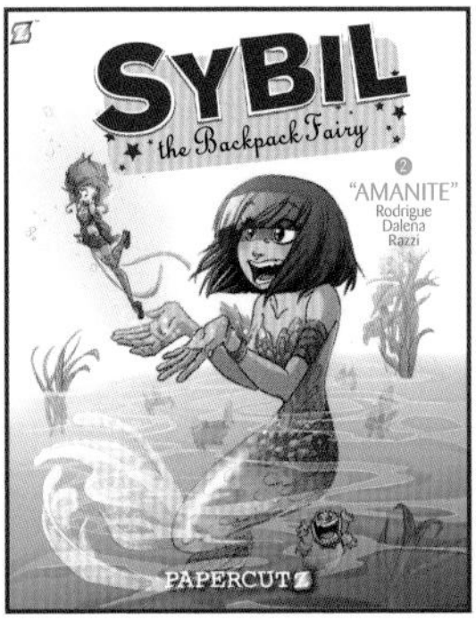
SYBIL
the Backpack Fairy
2 "AMANITE"
Rodrigue
Dalena
Razzi
PAPERCUTZ

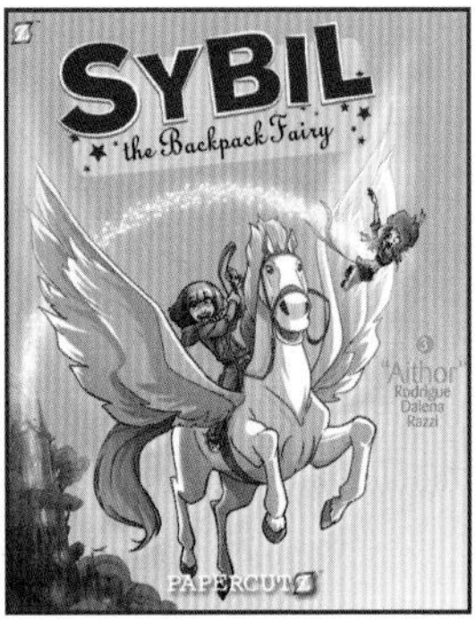
SYBIL
the Backpack Fairy
3 "Aithor"
Rodrigue
Dalena
Razzi
PAPERCUTZ

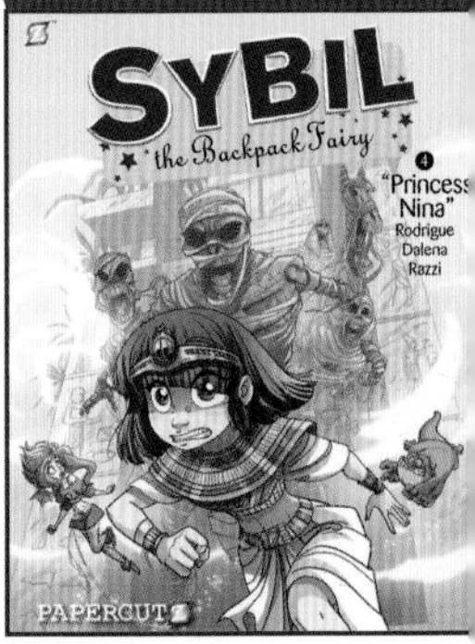
SYBIL
the Backpack Fairy
4 "Princess Nina"
Rodrigue
Dalena
Razzi
PAPERCUTZ

1 "NINA" 2 "AMANITE" 3 "AITHOR" 4 "PRINCESS NINA

SYBIL THE BACKPACK FAIRY graphic novels are available in hardcover for $10.99 each, except #2, for $11.99 from booksellers everywhere. You can also order online from www.papercutz.com. Or call 1-800-886-1223, Monday through Fridays, 9 – 5 EST. MC, Visa, and AmEx accepted. To order by mail, please add $4.00 for postage and handling for first book ordered, $1.00 for each additional book, and make check payable to NBM Publishing. Send to: Papercutz, 160 Broadway, Suite 700, East Wing, New York, NY 10038.

Sybil the Backpack Fairy
#3 "Aithor"
MICHEL RODRIGUE – Writer
ANTONELLO DALENA & MANUELA RAZZI – Artists
CECILIA GIUMENTO – Colorist
JOE JOHNSON – Translation
JANICE CHIANG – Lettering
JULIE SARTAIN – Production
MICHAEL PETRANEK – Associate Editor
JIM SALICRUP
Editor-in-Chief

ISBN: 978-1-59707-369-1

Printed in China
December 2012 by New Era Printing, LTD
Unit C, 8/F, Worldwide Centre
123 Tung Chau St
Kowloon, Hong Kong

Distributed by Macmillan
First Papercutz Printing

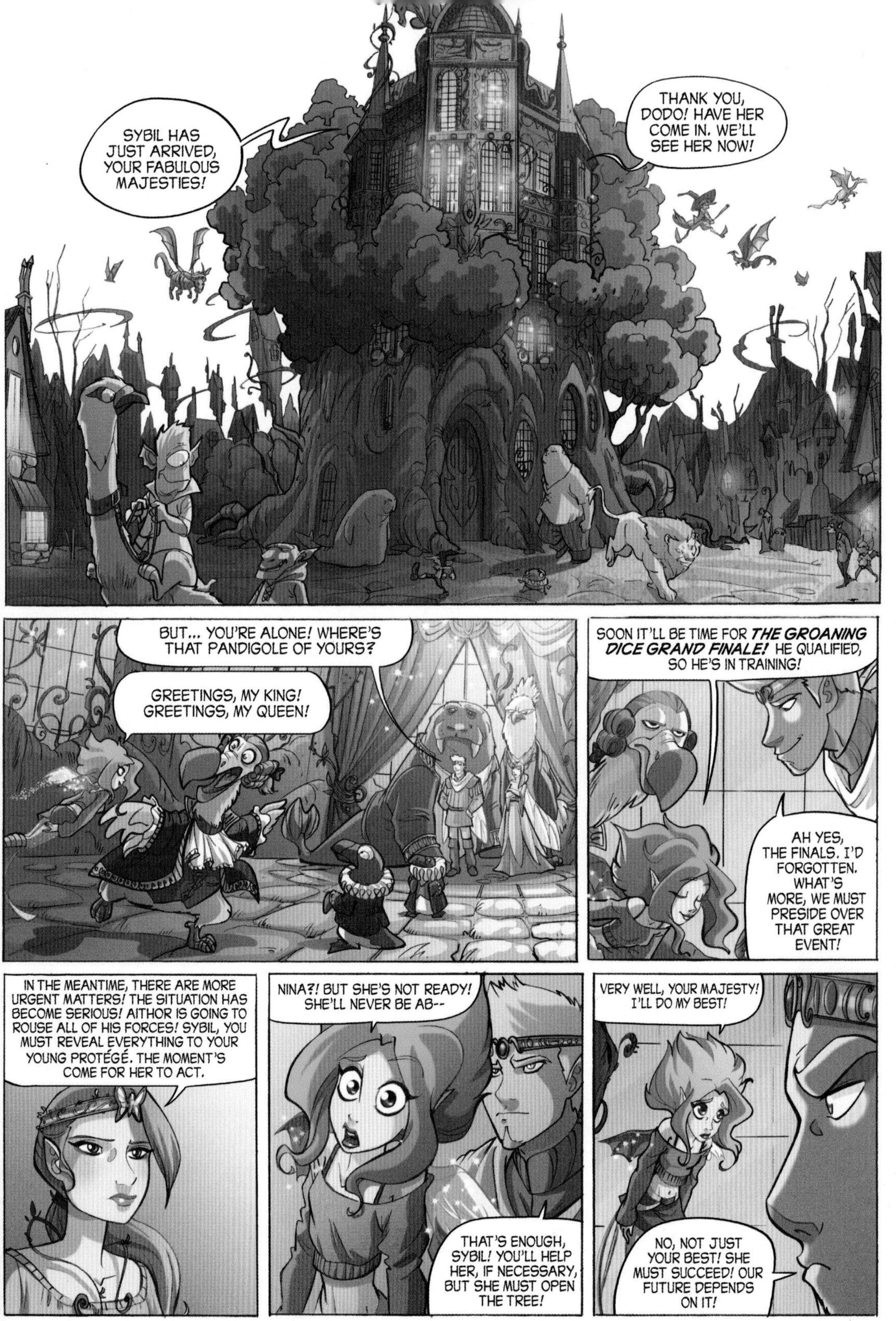
SYBIL HAS JUST ARRIVED, YOUR FABULOUS MAJESTIES!
THANK YOU, DODO! HAVE HER COME IN. WE'LL SEE HER NOW!
GREETINGS, MY KING! GREETINGS, MY QUEEN!
BUT... YOU'RE ALONE! WHERE'S THAT PANDIGOLE OF YOURS?
SOON IT'LL BE TIME FOR THE GROANING DICE GRAND FINALE! HE QUALIFIED, SO HE'S IN TRAINING!
AH YES, THE FINALS. I'D FORGOTTEN. WHAT'S MORE, WE MUST PRESIDE OVER THAT GREAT EVENT!
IN THE MEANTIME, THERE ARE MORE URGENT MATTERS! THE SITUATION HAS BECOME SERIOUS! AITHOR IS GOING TO ROUSE ALL OF HIS FORCES! SYBIL, YOU MUST REVEAL EVERYTHING TO YOUR YOUNG PROTÉGÉ. THE MOMENT'S COME FOR HER TO ACT.
NINA?! BUT SHE'S NOT READY! SHE'LL NEVER BE AB--
THAT'S ENOUGH, SYBIL! YOU'LL HELP HER, IF NECESSARY, BUT SHE MUST OPEN THE TREE!
VERY WELL, YOUR MAJESTY! I'LL DO MY BEST!
NO, NOT JUST YOUR BEST! SHE MUST SUCCEED! OUR FUTURE DEPENDS ON IT!

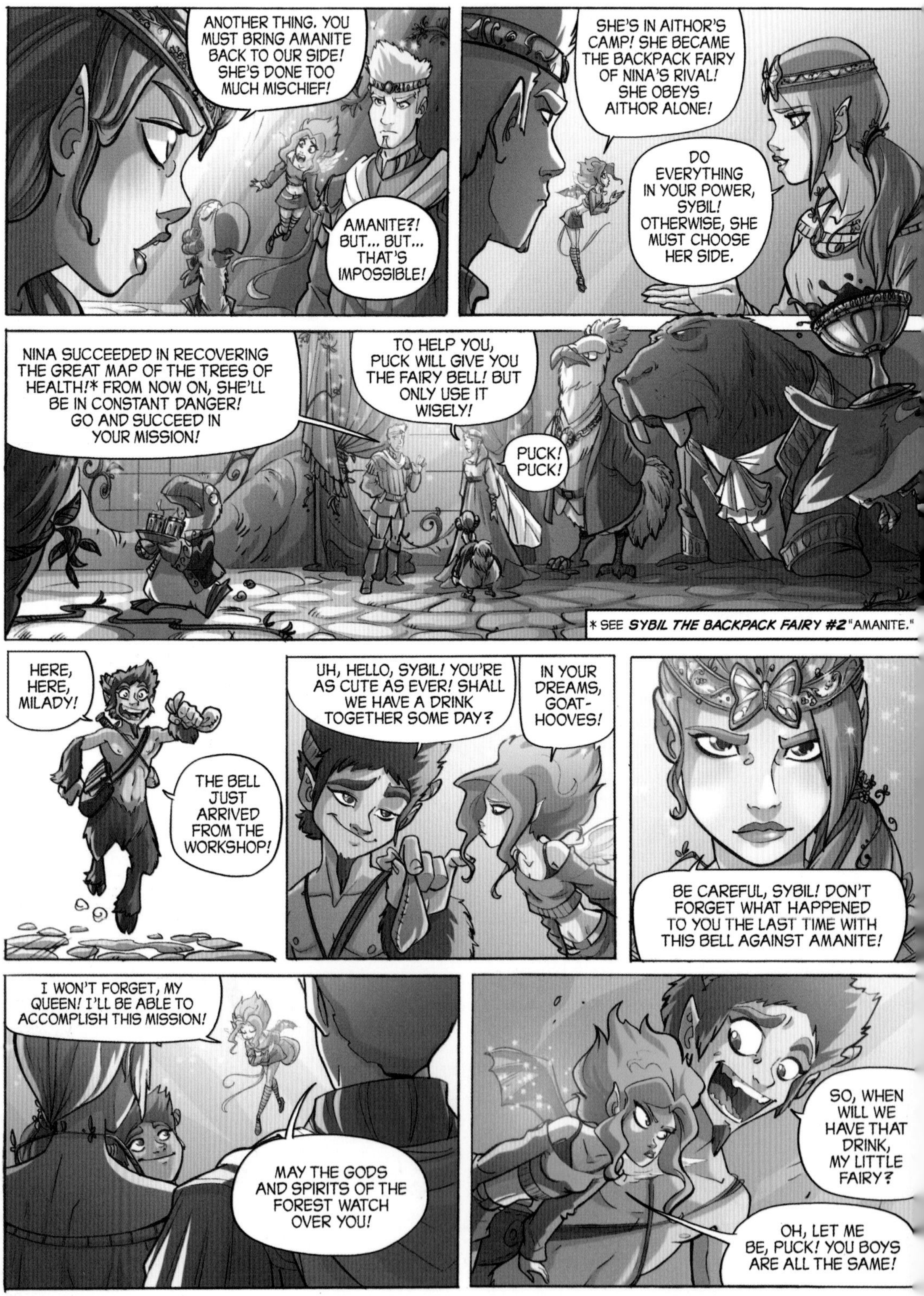
ANOTHER THING. YOU MUST BRING AMANITE BACK TO OUR SIDE! SHE'S DONE TOO MUCH MISCHIEF!
AMANITE?! BUT... BUT... THAT'S IMPOSSIBLE!
SHE'S IN AITHOR'S CAMP! SHE BECAME THE BACKPACK FAIRY OF NINA'S RIVAL! SHE OBEYS AITHOR ALONE!
DO EVERYTHING IN YOUR POWER, SYBIL! OTHERWISE, SHE MUST CHOOSE HER SIDE.
NINA SUCCEEDED IN RECOVERING THE GREAT MAP OF THE TREES OF HEALTH!* FROM NOW ON, SHE'LL BE IN CONSTANT DANGER! GO AND SUCCEED IN YOUR MISSION!
TO HELP YOU, PUCK WILL GIVE YOU THE FAIRY BELL! BUT ONLY USE IT WISELY!
PUCK! PUCK!
* SEE SYBIL THE BACKPACK FAIRY #2 "AMANITE."
HERE, HERE, MILADY!
THE BELL JUST ARRIVED FROM THE WORKSHOP!
UH, HELLO, SYBIL! YOU'RE AS CUTE AS EVER! SHALL WE HAVE A DRINK TOGETHER SOME DAY?
IN YOUR DREAMS, GOAT-HOOVES!
BE CAREFUL, SYBIL! DON'T FORGET WHAT HAPPENED TO YOU THE LAST TIME WITH THIS BELL AGAINST AMANITE!
I WON'T FORGET, MY QUEEN! I'LL BE ABLE TO ACCOMPLISH THIS MISSION!
MAY THE GODS AND SPIRITS OF THE FOREST WATCH OVER YOU!
SO, WHEN WILL WE HAVE THAT DRINK, MY LITTLE FAIRY?
OH, LET ME BE, PUCK! YOU BOYS ARE ALL THE SAME!

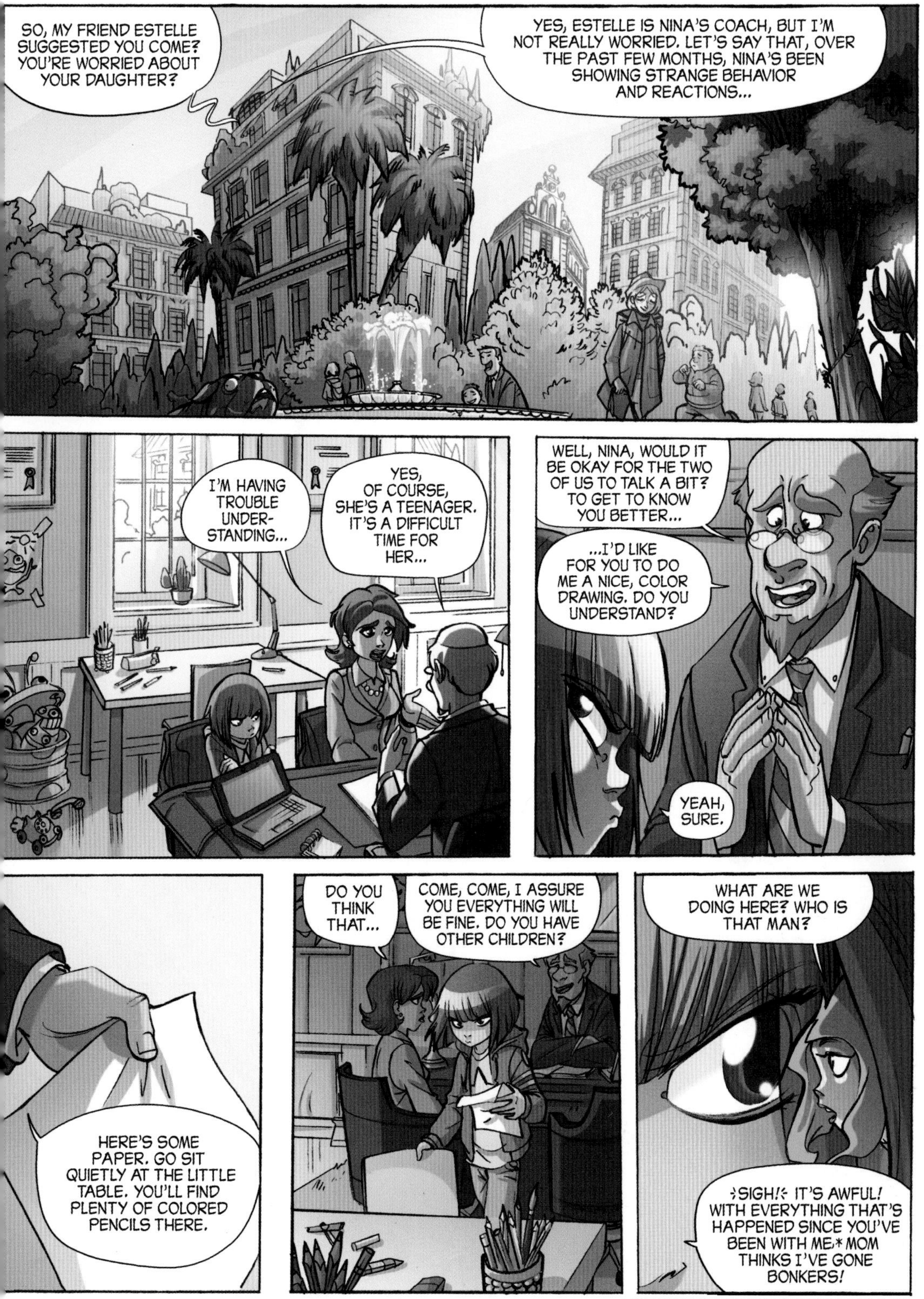
SO, MY FRIEND ESTELLE SUGGESTED YOU COME? YOU'RE WORRIED ABOUT YOUR DAUGHTER?
YES, ESTELLE IS NINA'S COACH, BUT I'M NOT REALLY WORRIED. LET'S SAY THAT, OVER THE PAST FEW MONTHS, NINA'S BEEN SHOWING STRANGE BEHAVIOR AND REACTIONS...
I'M HAVING TROUBLE UNDER-STANDING...
YES, OF COURSE, SHE'S A TEENAGER. IT'S A DIFFICULT TIME FOR HER...
WELL, NINA, WOULD IT BE OKAY FOR THE TWO OF US TO TALK A BIT? TO GET TO KNOW YOU BETTER...
...I'D LIKE FOR YOU TO DO ME A NICE, COLOR DRAWING. DO YOU UNDERSTAND?
YEAH, SURE.
HERE'S SOME PAPER. GO SIT QUIETLY AT THE LITTLE TABLE. YOU'LL FIND PLENTY OF COLORED PENCILS THERE.
DO YOU THINK THAT...
COME, COME, I ASSURE YOU EVERYTHING WILL BE FINE. DO YOU HAVE OTHER CHILDREN?
WHAT ARE WE DOING HERE? WHO IS THAT MAN?
SIGH! IT'S AWFUL! WITH EVERYTHING THAT'S HAPPENED SINCE YOU'VE BEEN WITH ME,* MOM THINKS I'VE GONE BONKERS!

* SEE *SYBIL THE BACKPACKFAIRY #1 & #2.*

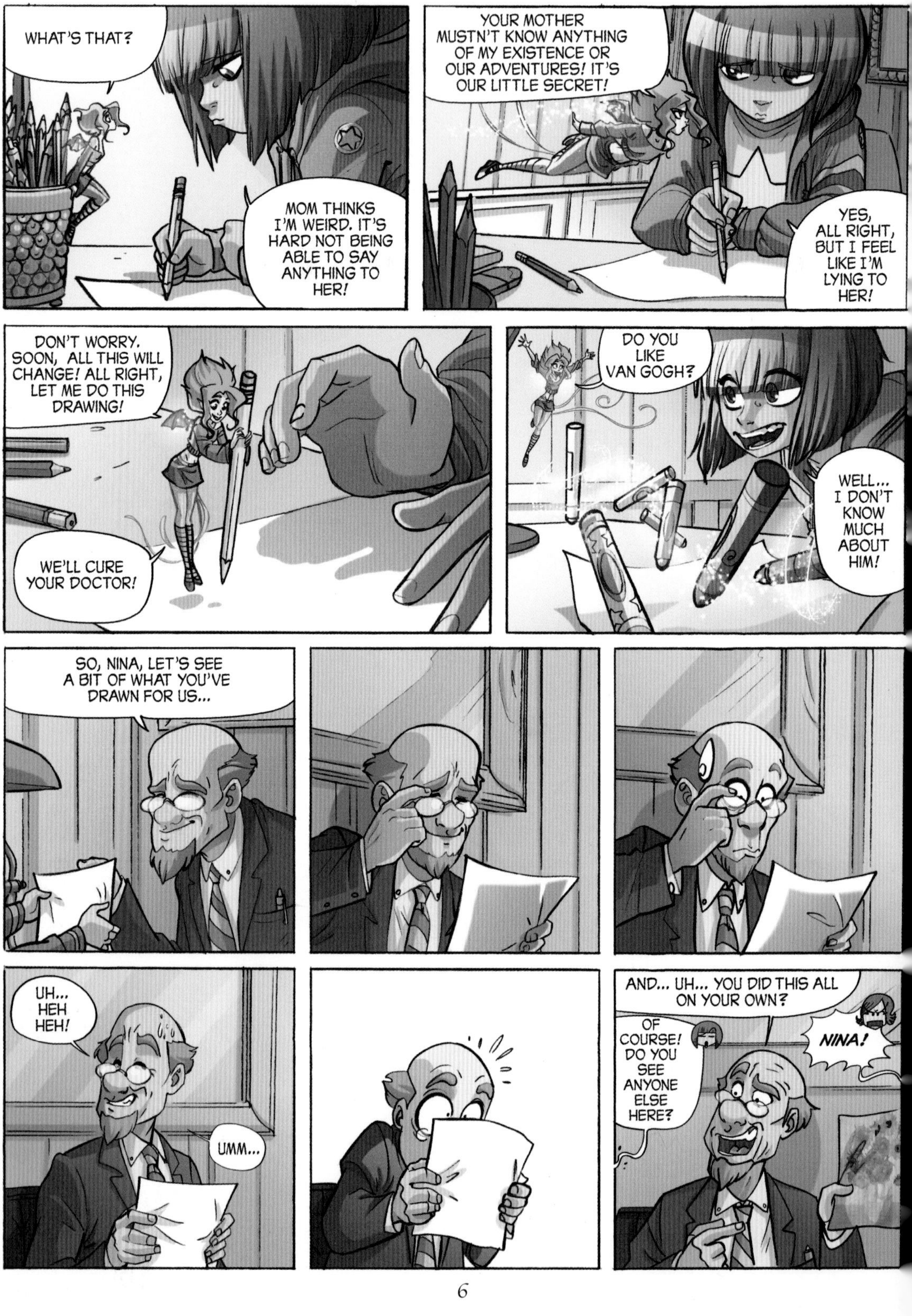
WHAT'S THAT?
MOM THINKS I'M WEIRD. IT'S HARD NOT BEING ABLE TO SAY ANYTHING TO HER!
YOUR MOTHER MUSTN'T KNOW ANYTHING OF MY EXISTENCE OR OUR ADVENTURES! IT'S OUR LITTLE SECRET!
YES, ALL RIGHT, BUT I FEEL LIKE I'M LYING TO HER!
DON'T WORRY. SOON, ALL THIS WILL CHANGE! ALL RIGHT, LET ME DO THIS DRAWING!
WE'LL CURE YOUR DOCTOR!
DO YOU LIKE VAN GOGH?
WELL... I DON'T KNOW MUCH ABOUT HIM!
SO, NINA, LET'S SEE A BIT OF WHAT YOU'VE DRAWN FOR US...
UH... HEH HEH!
UMM...
AND... UH... YOU DID THIS ALL ON YOUR OWN?
OF COURSE! DO YOU SEE ANYONE ELSE HERE?
NINA!

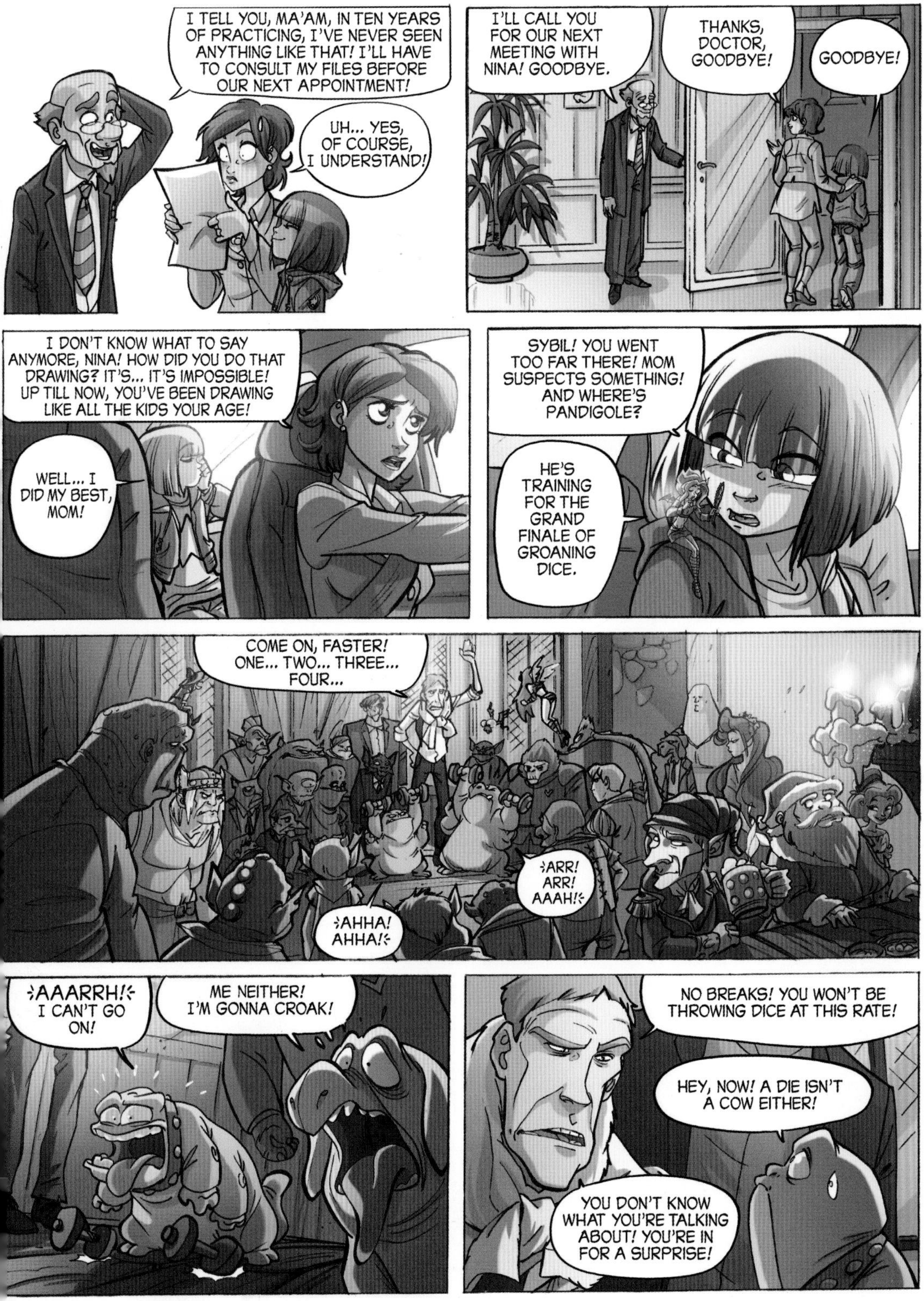
I TELL YOU, MA'AM, IN TEN YEARS OF PRACTICING, I'VE NEVER SEEN ANYTHING LIKE THAT! I'LL HAVE TO CONSULT MY FILES BEFORE OUR NEXT APPOINTMENT!
UH... YES, OF COURSE, I UNDERSTAND!
I'LL CALL YOU FOR OUR NEXT MEETING WITH NINA! GOODBYE.
THANKS, DOCTOR, GOODBYE!
GOODBYE!
I DON'T KNOW WHAT TO SAY ANYMORE, NINA! HOW DID YOU DO THAT DRAWING? IT'S... IT'S IMPOSSIBLE! UP TILL NOW, YOU'VE BEEN DRAWING LIKE ALL THE KIDS YOUR AGE!
WELL... I DID MY BEST, MOM!
SYBIL! YOU WENT TOO FAR THERE! MOM SUSPECTS SOMETHING! AND WHERE'S PANDIGOLE?
HE'S TRAINING FOR THE GRAND FINALE OF GROANING DICE.
COME ON, FASTER! ONE... TWO... THREE... FOUR...
ARR! ARR! AAAH!
AHHA! AHHA!
AAARRH! I CAN'T GO ON!
ME NEITHER! I'M GONNA CROAK!
NO BREAKS! YOU WON'T BE THROWING DICE AT THIS RATE!
HEY, NOW! A DIE ISN'T A COW EITHER!
YOU DON'T KNOW WHAT YOU'RE TALKING ABOUT! YOU'RE IN FOR A SURPRISE!

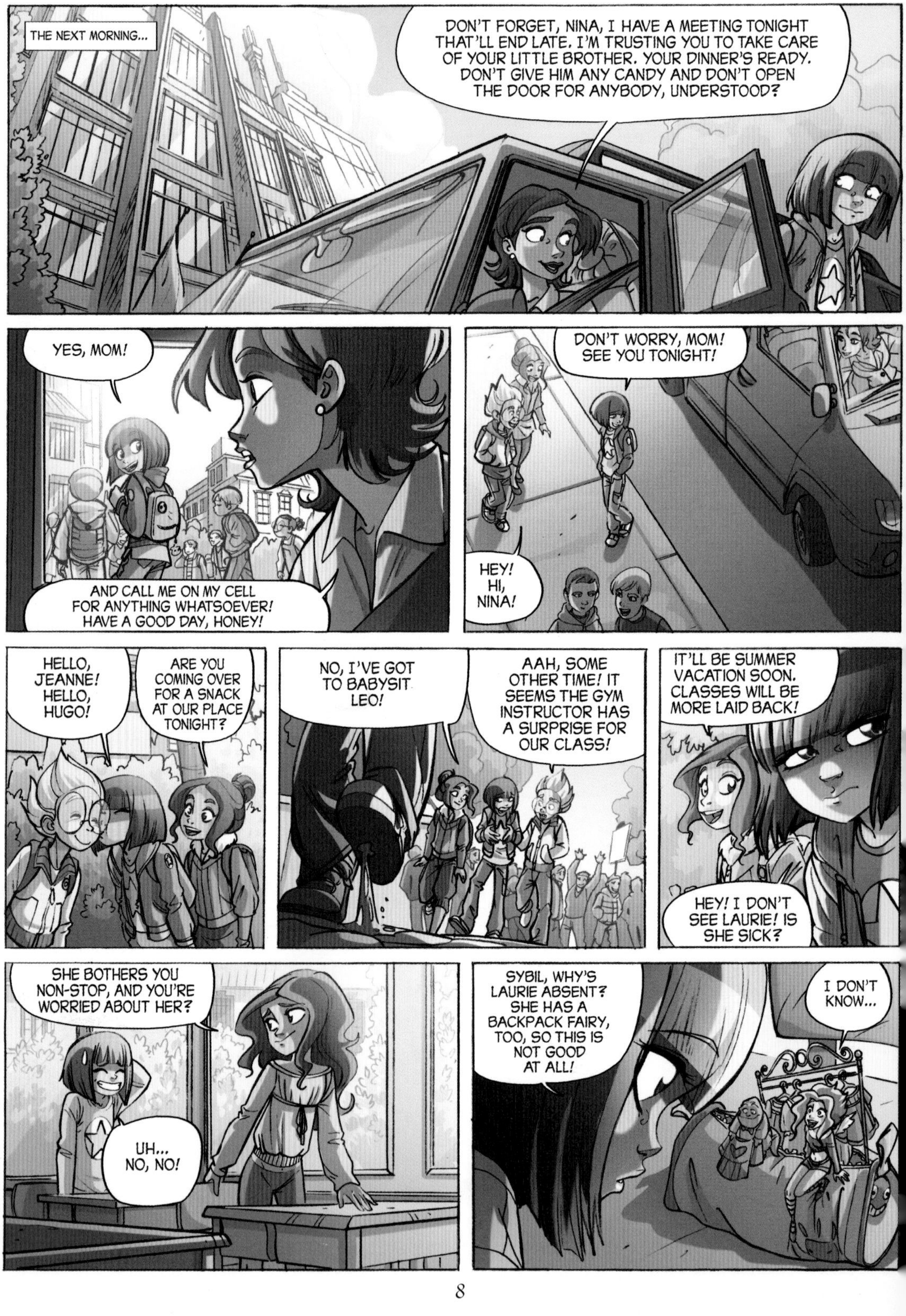

THE NEXT MORNING...
DON'T FORGET, NINA, I HAVE A MEETING TONIGHT THAT'LL END LATE. I'M TRUSTING YOU TO TAKE CARE OF YOUR LITTLE BROTHER. YOUR DINNER'S READY. DON'T GIVE HIM ANY CANDY AND DON'T OPEN THE DOOR FOR ANYBODY, UNDERSTOOD?
YES, MOM!
AND CALL ME ON MY CELL FOR ANYTHING WHATSOEVER! HAVE A GOOD DAY, HONEY!
DON'T WORRY, MOM! SEE YOU TONIGHT!
HEY! HI, NINA!
HELLO, JEANNE! HELLO, HUGO!
ARE YOU COMING OVER FOR A SNACK AT OUR PLACE TONIGHT?
NO, I'VE GOT TO BABYSIT LEO!
AAH, SOME OTHER TIME! IT SEEMS THE GYM INSTRUCTOR HAS A SURPRISE FOR OUR CLASS!
IT'LL BE SUMMER VACATION SOON. CLASSES WILL BE MORE LAID BACK!
HEY! I DON'T SEE LAURIE! IS SHE SICK?
SHE BOTHERS YOU NON-STOP, AND YOU'RE WORRIED ABOUT HER?
UH... NO, NO!
SYBIL, WHY'S LAURIE ABSENT? SHE HAS A BACKPACK FAIRY, TOO, SO THIS IS NOT GOOD AT ALL!
I DON'T KNOW...

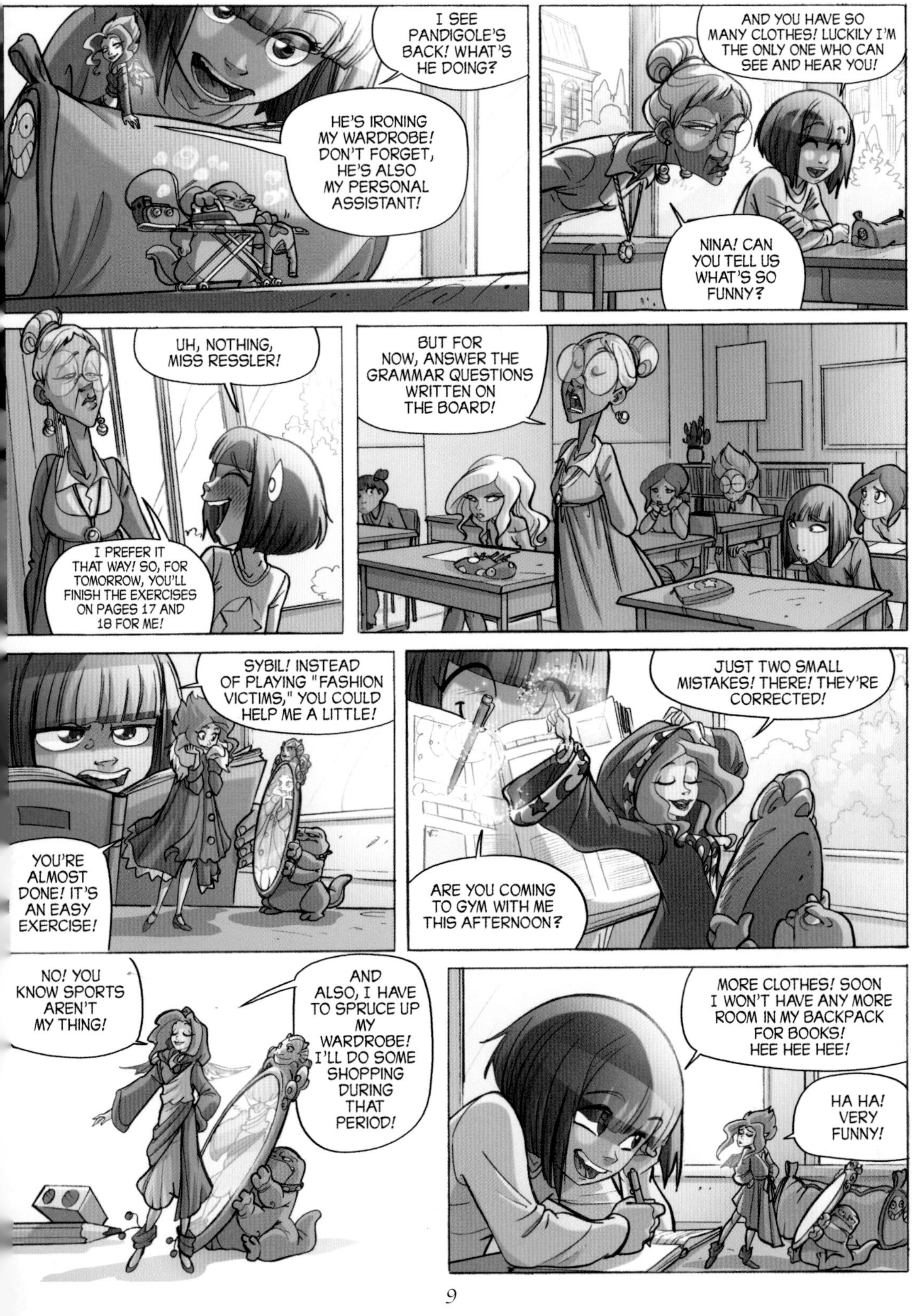
I SEE PANDIGOLE'S BACK! WHAT'S HE DOING?
HE'S IRONING MY WARDROBE! DON'T FORGET, HE'S ALSO MY PERSONAL ASSISTANT!
AND YOU HAVE SO MANY CLOTHES! LUCKILY I'M THE ONLY ONE WHO CAN SEE AND HEAR YOU!
NINA! CAN YOU TELL US WHAT'S SO FUNNY?
UH, NOTHING, MISS RESSLER!
I PREFER IT THAT WAY! SO, FOR TOMORROW, YOU'LL FINISH THE EXERCISES ON PAGES 17 AND 18 FOR ME!
BUT FOR NOW, ANSWER THE GRAMMAR QUESTIONS WRITTEN ON THE BOARD!
SYBIL! INSTEAD OF PLAYING "FASHION VICTIMS," YOU COULD HELP ME A LITTLE!
YOU'RE ALMOST DONE! IT'S AN EASY EXERCISE!
JUST TWO SMALL MISTAKES! THERE! THEY'RE CORRECTED!
ARE YOU COMING TO GYM WITH ME THIS AFTERNOON?
NO! YOU KNOW SPORTS AREN'T MY THING!
AND ALSO, I HAVE TO SPRUCE UP MY WARDROBE! I'LL DO SOME SHOPPING DURING THAT PERIOD!
MORE CLOTHES! SOON I WON'T HAVE ANY MORE ROOM IN MY BACKPACK FOR BOOKS! HEE HEE HEE!
HA HA! VERY FUNNY!

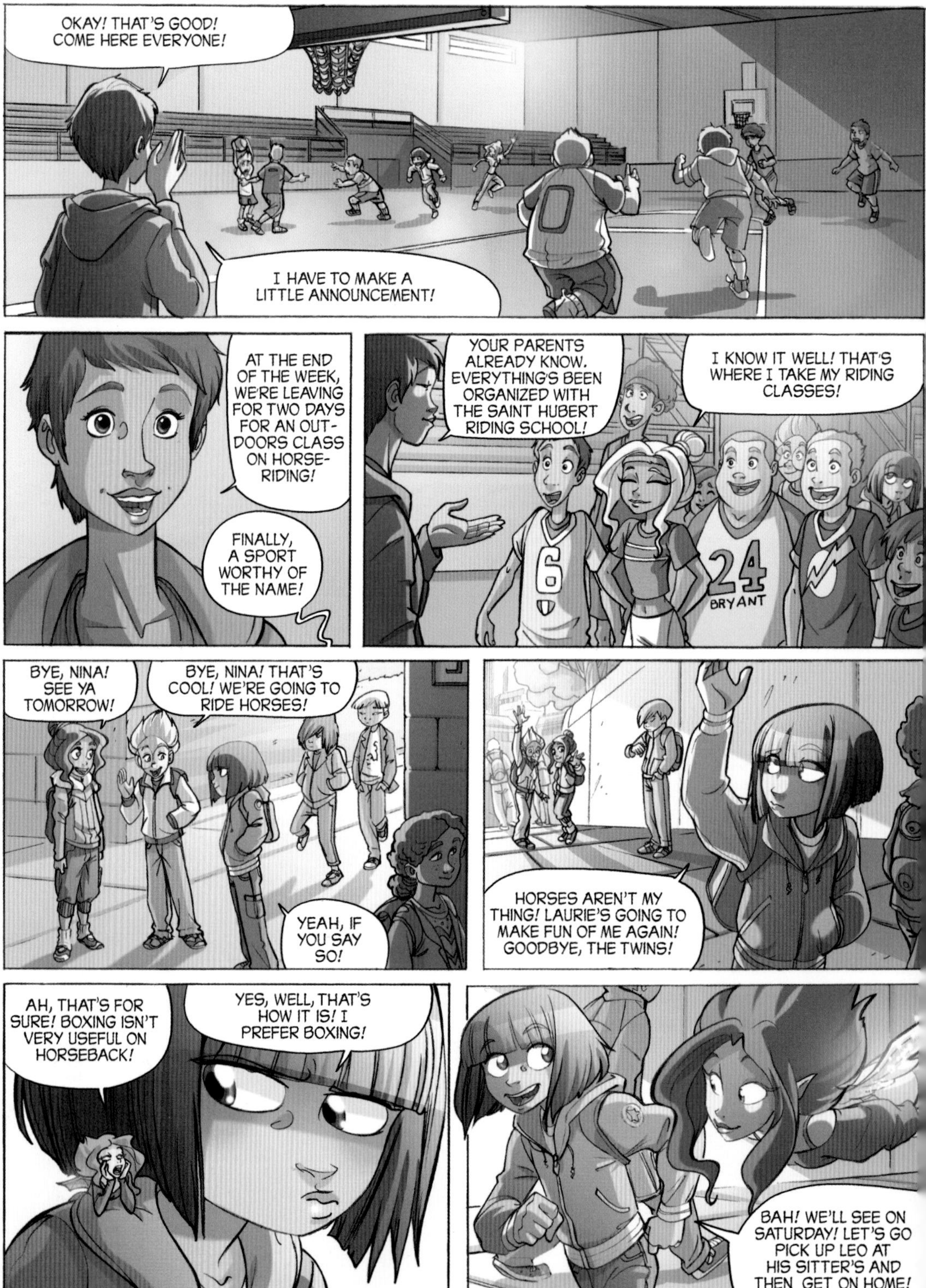
OKAY! THAT'S GOOD! COME HERE EVERYONE!
I HAVE TO MAKE A LITTLE ANNOUNCEMENT!
AT THE END OF THE WEEK, WE'RE LEAVING FOR TWO DAYS FOR AN OUT-DOORS CLASS ON HORSE-RIDING!
FINALLY, A SPORT WORTHY OF THE NAME!
YOUR PARENTS ALREADY KNOW. EVERYTHING'S BEEN ORGANIZED WITH THE SAINT HUBERT RIDING SCHOOL!
I KNOW IT WELL! THAT'S WHERE I TAKE MY RIDING CLASSES!
6
24
BRYANT
BYE, NINA! SEE YA TOMORROW!
BYE, NINA! THAT'S COOL! WE'RE GOING TO RIDE HORSES!
YEAH, IF YOU SAY SO!
HORSES AREN'T MY THING! LAURIE'S GOING TO MAKE FUN OF ME AGAIN! GOODBYE, THE TWINS!
AH, THAT'S FOR SURE! BOXING ISN'T VERY USEFUL ON HORSEBACK!
YES, WELL, THAT'S HOW IT IS! I PREFER BOXING!
BAH! WE'LL SEE ON SATURDAY! LET'S GO PICK UP LEO AT HIS SITTER'S AND THEN GET ON HOME!

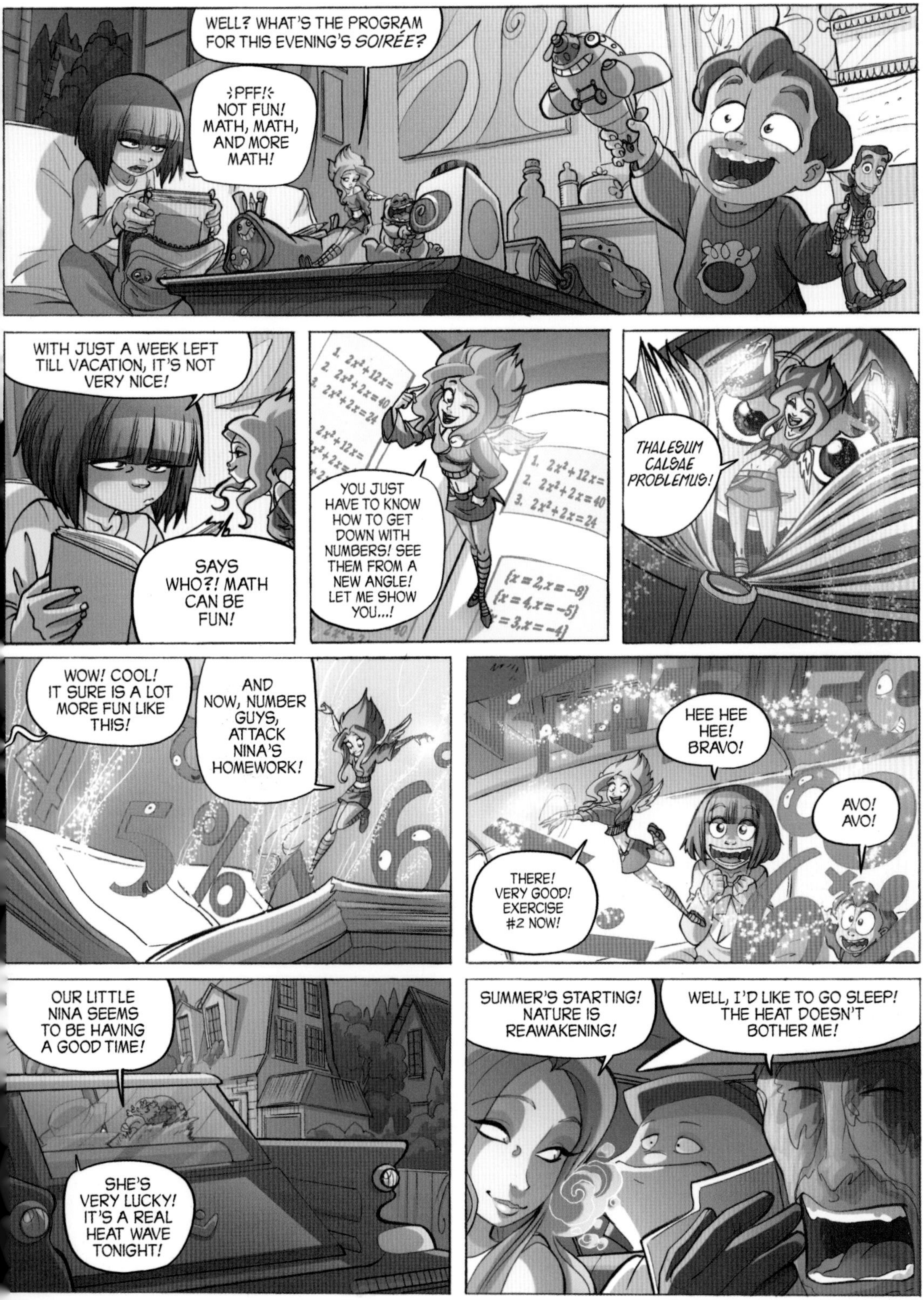
WELL? WHAT'S THE PROGRAM FOR THIS EVENING'S SOIRÉE?
PFF! NOT FUN! MATH, MATH, AND MORE MATH!
WITH JUST A WEEK LEFT TILL VACATION, IT'S NOT VERY NICE!
SAYS WHO?! MATH CAN BE FUN!
YOU JUST HAVE TO KNOW HOW TO GET DOWN WITH NUMBERS! SEE THEM FROM A NEW ANGLE! LET ME SHOW YOU...!
THALESUM CALSAE PROBLEMUS!
WOW! COOL! IT SURE IS A LOT MORE FUN LIKE THIS!
AND NOW, NUMBER GUYS, ATTACK NINA'S HOMEWORK!
HEE HEE HEE! BRAVO!
AVO! AVO!
THERE! VERY GOOD! EXERCISE #2 NOW!
OUR LITTLE NINA SEEMS TO BE HAVING A GOOD TIME!
SHE'S VERY LUCKY! IT'S A REAL HEAT WAVE TONIGHT!
SUMMER'S STARTING! NATURE IS REAWAKENING!
WELL, I'D LIKE TO GO SLEEP! THE HEAT DOESN'T BOTHER ME!

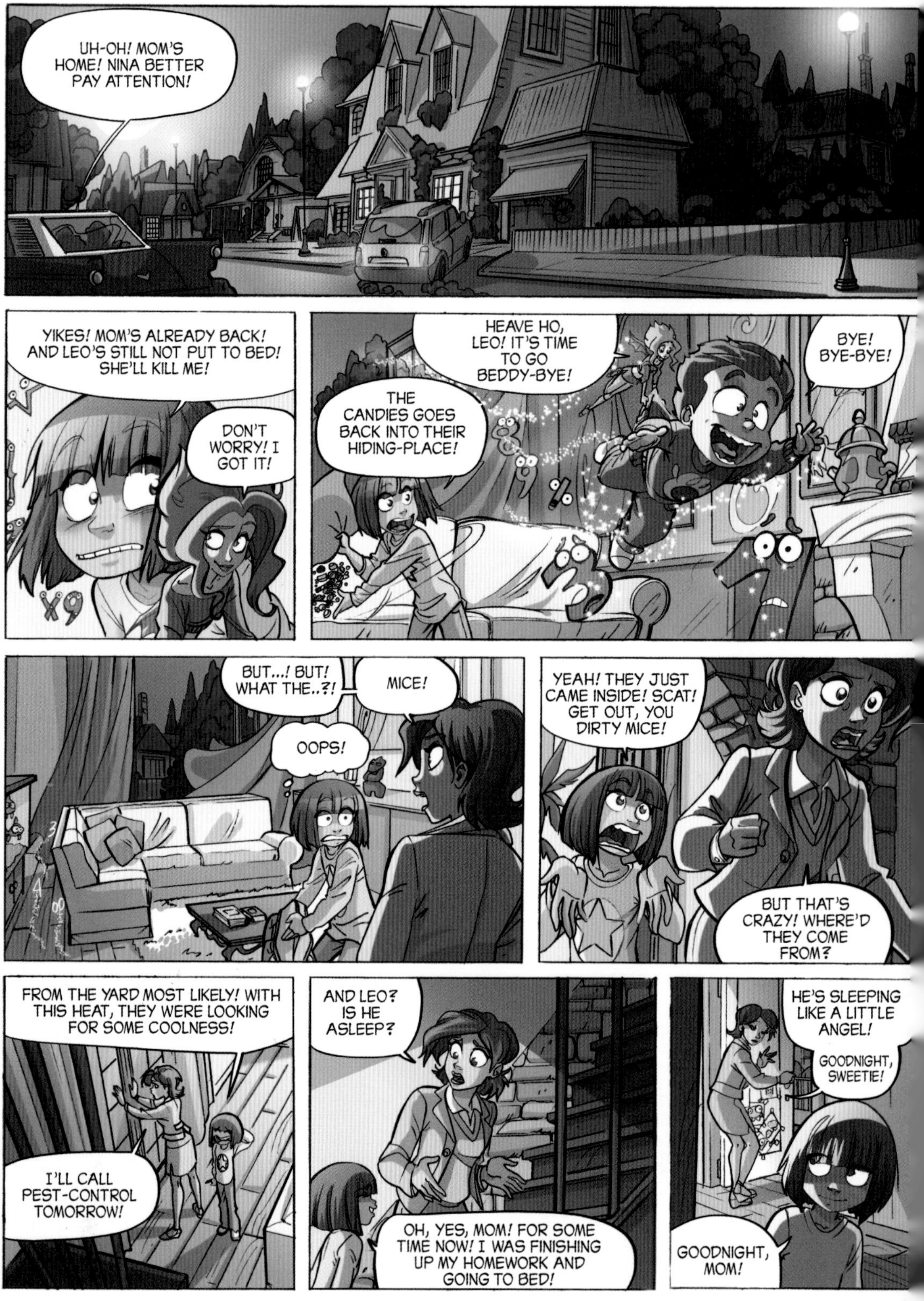
UH-OH! MOM'S HOME! NINA BETTER PAY ATTENTION!
YIKES! MOM'S ALREADY BACK! AND LEO'S STILL NOT PUT TO BED! SHE'LL KILL ME!
DON'T WORRY! I GOT IT!
HEAVE HO, LEO! IT'S TIME TO GO BEDDY-BYE!
THE CANDIES GOES BACK INTO THEIR HIDING-PLACE!
BYE! BYE-BYE!
BUT...! BUT! WHAT THE..?!
MICE!
OOPS!
YEAH! THEY JUST CAME INSIDE! SCAT! GET OUT, YOU DIRTY MICE!
BUT THAT'S CRAZY! WHERE'D THEY COME FROM?
FROM THE YARD MOST LIKELY! WITH THIS HEAT, THEY WERE LOOKING FOR SOME COOLNESS!
I'LL CALL PEST-CONTROL TOMORROW!
AND LEO? IS HE ASLEEP?
OH, YES, MOM! FOR SOME TIME NOW! I WAS FINISHING UP MY HOMEWORK AND GOING TO BED!
HE'S SLEEPING LIKE A LITTLE ANGEL!
GOODNIGHT, SWEETIE!
GOODNIGHT, MOM!

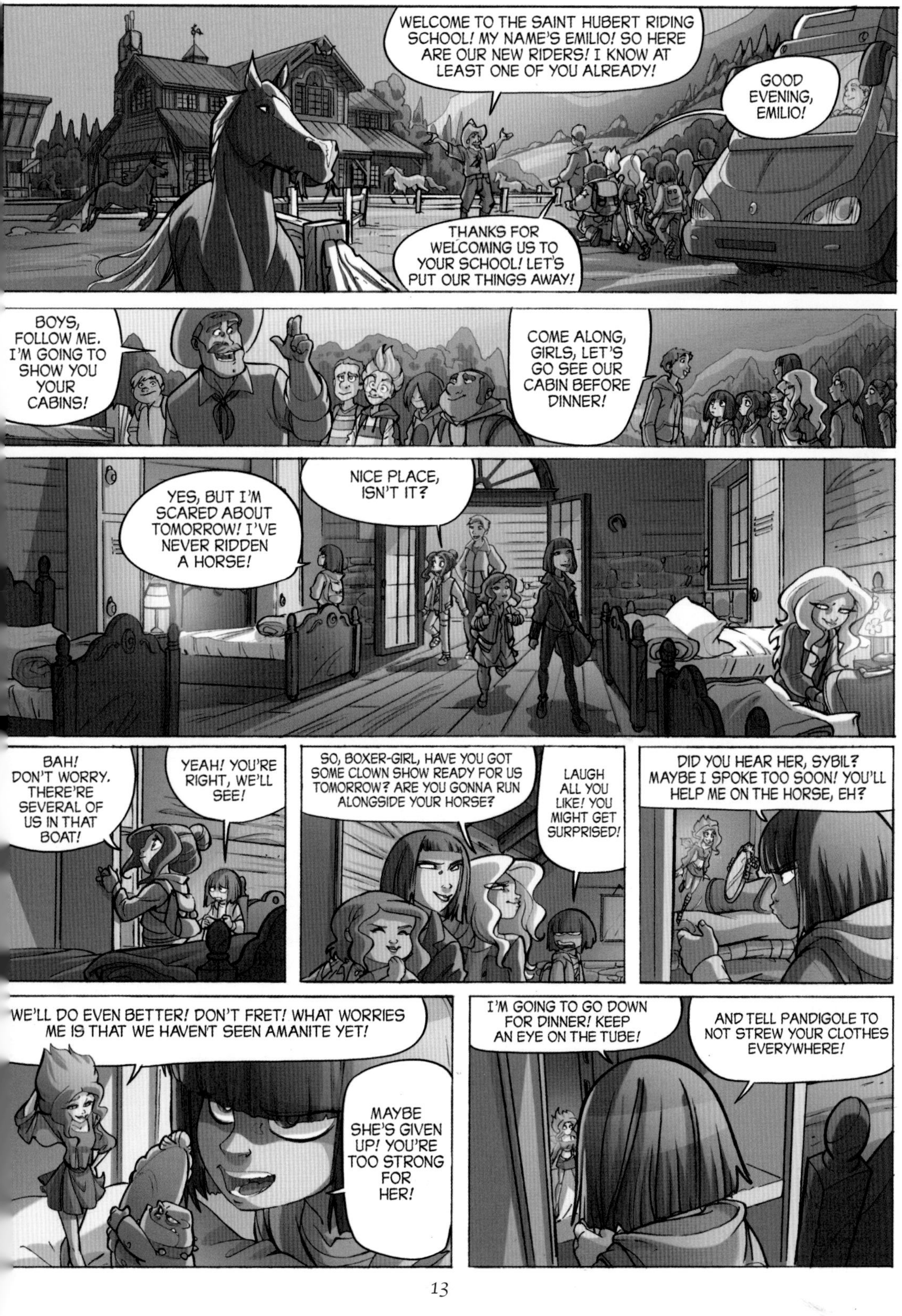
WELCOME TO THE SAINT HUBERT RIDING SCHOOL! MY NAME'S EMILIO! SO HERE ARE OUR NEW RIDERS! I KNOW AT LEAST ONE OF YOU ALREADY!
GOOD EVENING, EMILIO!
THANKS FOR WELCOMING US TO YOUR SCHOOL! LET'S PUT OUR THINGS AWAY!
BOYS, FOLLOW ME. I'M GOING TO SHOW YOU YOUR CABINS!
COME ALONG, GIRLS, LET'S GO SEE OUR CABIN BEFORE DINNER!
YES, BUT I'M SCARED ABOUT TOMORROW! I'VE NEVER RIDDEN A HORSE!
NICE PLACE, ISN'T IT?
BAH! DON'T WORRY. THERE'RE SEVERAL OF US IN THAT BOAT!
YEAH! YOU'RE RIGHT, WE'LL SEE!
SO, BOXER-GIRL, HAVE YOU GOT SOME CLOWN SHOW READY FOR US TOMORROW? ARE YOU GONNA RUN ALONGSIDE YOUR HORSE?
LAUGH ALL YOU LIKE! YOU MIGHT GET SURPRISED!
DID YOU HEAR HER, SYBIL? MAYBE I SPOKE TOO SOON! YOU'LL HELP ME ON THE HORSE, EH?
WE'LL DO EVEN BETTER! DON'T FRET! WHAT WORRIES ME IS THAT WE HAVEN'T SEEN AMANITE YET!
MAYBE SHE'S GIVEN UP! YOU'RE TOO STRONG FOR HER!
I'M GOING TO GO DOWN FOR DINNER! KEEP AN EYE ON THE TUBE!
AND TELL PANDIGOLE TO NOT STREW YOUR CLOTHES EVERYWHERE!

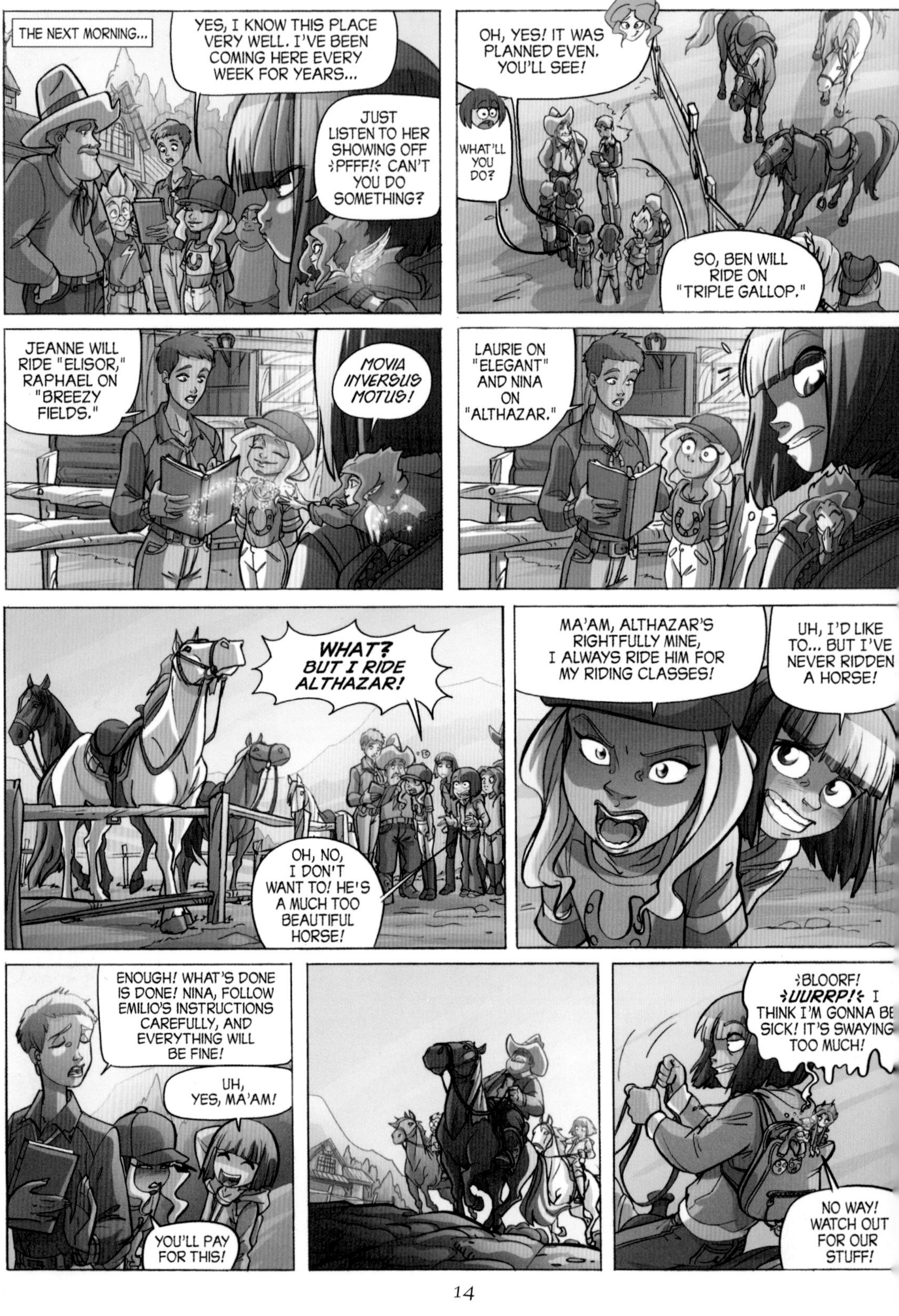
THE NEXT MORNING...
YES, I KNOW THIS PLACE VERY WELL. I'VE BEEN COMING HERE EVERY WEEK FOR YEARS...
JUST LISTEN TO HER SHOWING OFF *PFFF!* CAN'T YOU DO SOMETHING?
OH, YES! IT WAS PLANNED EVEN. YOU'LL SEE!
WHAT'LL YOU DO?
SO, BEN WILL RIDE ON "TRIPLE GALLOP."
JEANNE WILL RIDE "ELISOR," RAPHAEL ON "BREEZY FIELDS."
MOVIA INVERSUS MOTUS!
LAURIE ON "ELEGANT" AND NINA ON "ALTHAZAR."
WHAT? BUT I RIDE ALTHAZAR!
OH, NO, I DON'T WANT TO! HE'S A MUCH TOO BEAUTIFUL HORSE!
MA'AM, ALTHAZAR'S RIGHTFULLY MINE, I ALWAYS RIDE HIM FOR MY RIDING CLASSES!
UH, I'D LIKE TO... BUT I'VE NEVER RIDDEN A HORSE!
ENOUGH! WHAT'S DONE IS DONE! NINA, FOLLOW EMILIO'S INSTRUCTIONS CAREFULLY, AND EVERYTHING WILL BE FINE!
UH, YES, MA'AM!
YOU'LL PAY FOR THIS!
BLOORF! UURRP! I THINK I'M GONNA BE SICK! IT'S SWAYING TOO MUCH!
NO WAY! WATCH OUT FOR OUR STUFF!

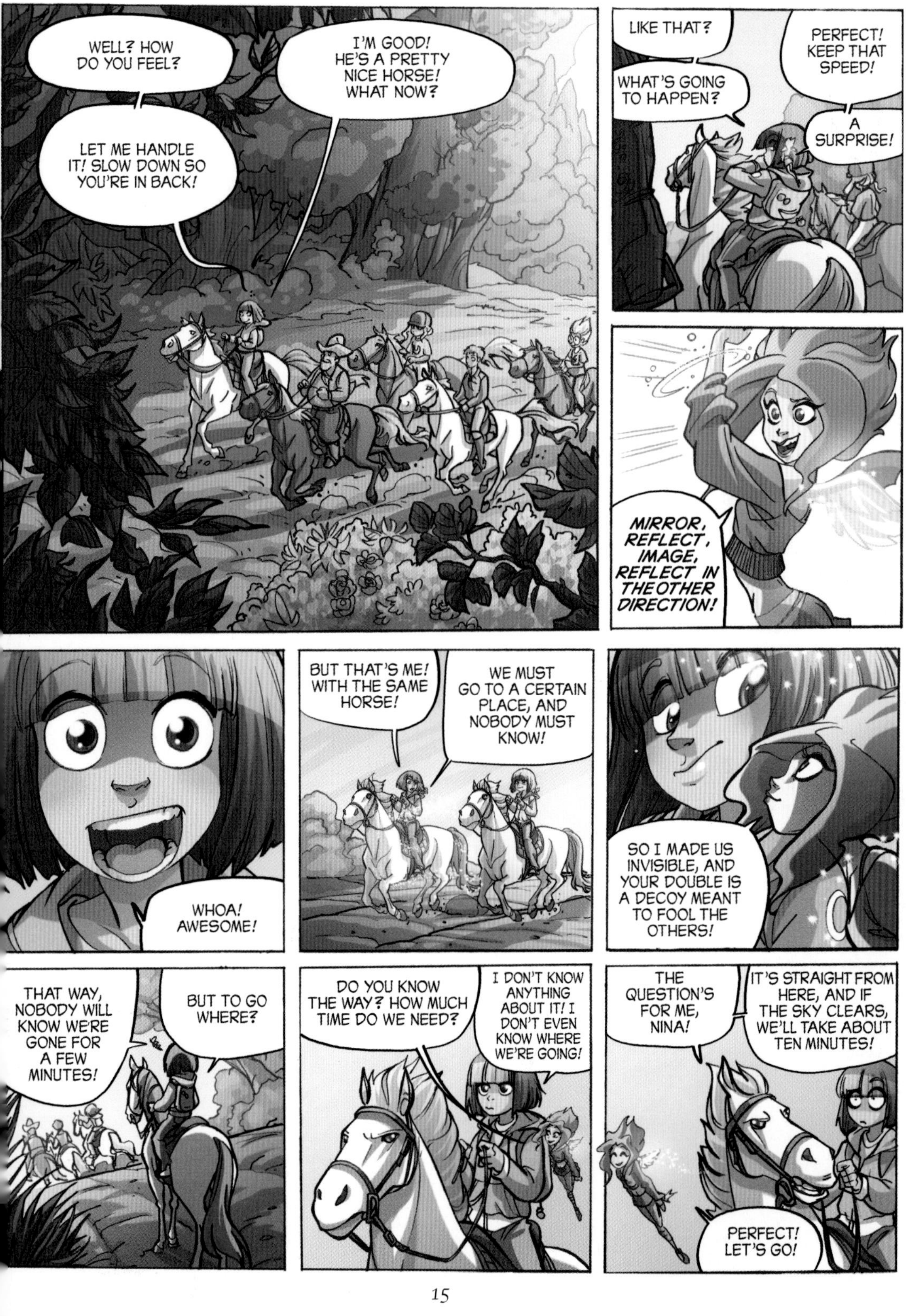
WELL? HOW DO YOU FEEL?
LET ME HANDLE IT! SLOW DOWN SO YOU'RE IN BACK!
I'M GOOD! HE'S A PRETTY NICE HORSE! WHAT NOW?
LIKE THAT?
WHAT'S GOING TO HAPPEN?
PERFECT! KEEP THAT SPEED!
A SURPRISE!
MIRROR, REFLECT, IMAGE, REFLECT IN THE OTHER DIRECTION!
WHOA! AWESOME!
BUT THAT'S ME! WITH THE SAME HORSE!
WE MUST GO TO A CERTAIN PLACE, AND NOBODY MUST KNOW!
SO I MADE US INVISIBLE, AND YOUR DOUBLE IS A DECOY MEANT TO FOOL THE OTHERS!
THAT WAY, NOBODY WILL KNOW WE'RE GONE FOR A FEW MINUTES!
BUT TO GO WHERE?
DO YOU KNOW THE WAY? HOW MUCH TIME DO WE NEED?
I DON'T KNOW ANYTHING ABOUT IT! I DON'T EVEN KNOW WHERE WE'RE GOING!
THE QUESTION'S FOR ME, NINA!
IT'S STRAIGHT FROM HERE, AND IF THE SKY CLEARS, WE'LL TAKE ABOUT TEN MINUTES!
PERFECT! LET'S GO!

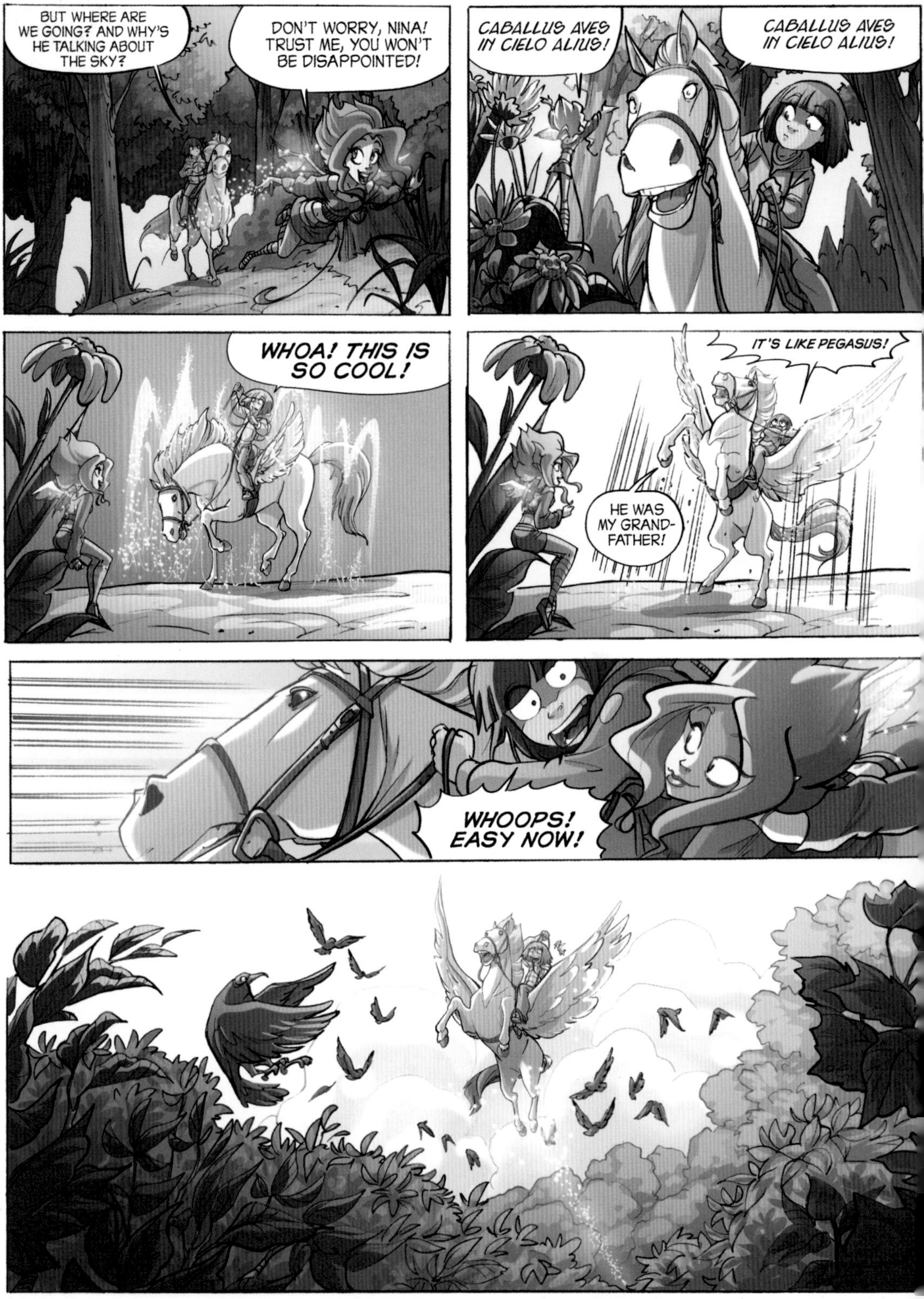
BUT WHERE ARE WE GOING? AND WHY'S HE TALKING ABOUT THE SKY?
DON'T WORRY, NINA! TRUST ME, YOU WON'T BE DISAPPOINTED!
CABALLUS AVES IN CIELO ALIUS!
CABALLUS AVES IN CIELO ALIUS!
WHOA! THIS IS SO COOL!
IT'S LIKE PEGASUS!
HE WAS MY GRAND-FATHER!
WHOOPS! EASY NOW!

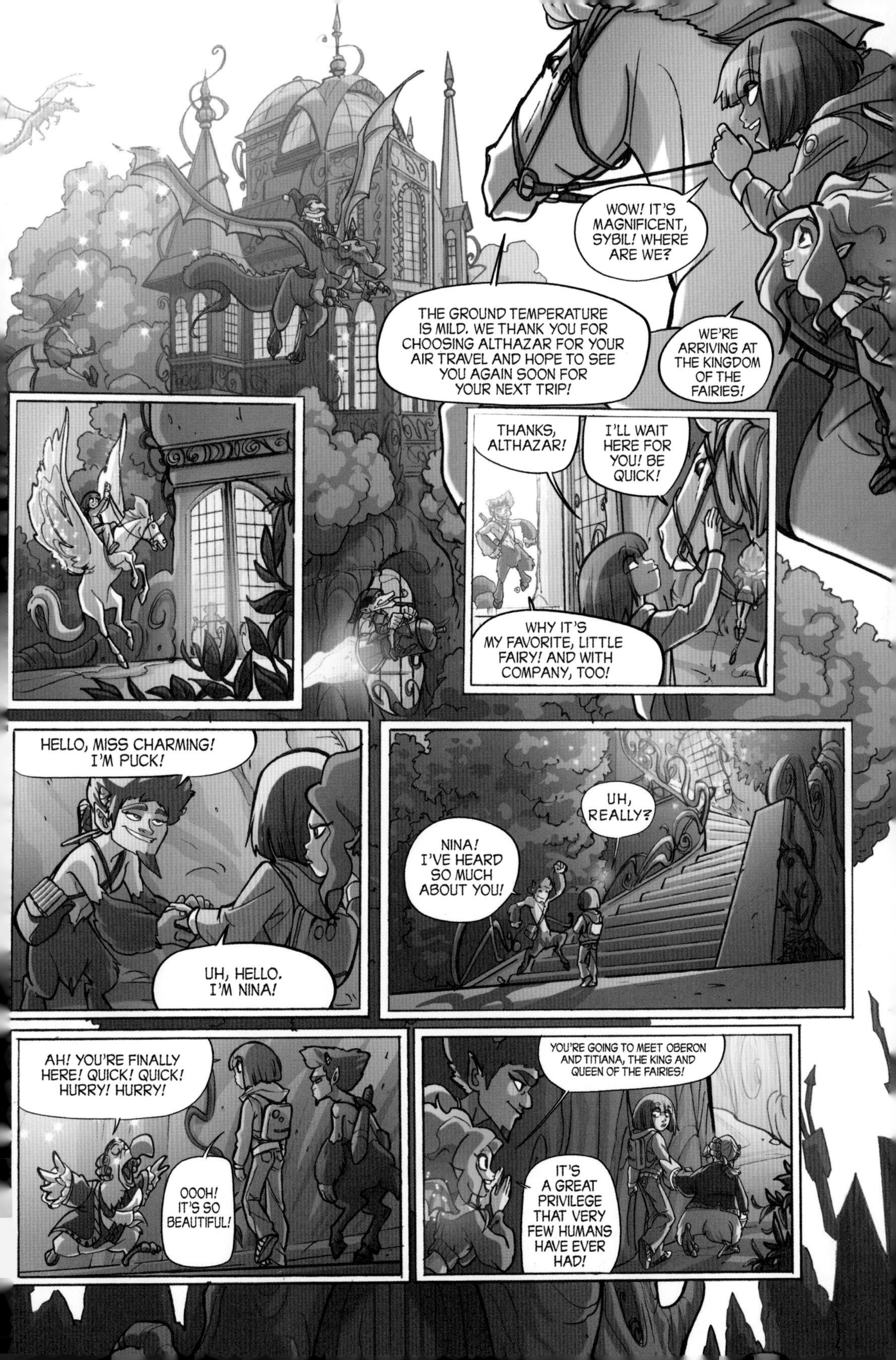
WOW! IT'S MAGNIFICENT, SYBIL! WHERE ARE WE?
THE GROUND TEMPERATURE IS MILD. WE THANK YOU FOR CHOOSING ALTHAZAR FOR YOUR AIR TRAVEL AND HOPE TO SEE YOU AGAIN SOON FOR YOUR NEXT TRIP!
WE'RE ARRIVING AT THE KINGDOM OF THE FAIRIES!
THANKS, ALTHAZAR!
I'LL WAIT HERE FOR YOU! BE QUICK!
WHY IT'S MY FAVORITE, LITTLE FAIRY! AND WITH COMPANY, TOO!
HELLO, MISS CHARMING! I'M PUCK!
UH, HELLO. I'M NINA!
NINA! I'VE HEARD SO MUCH ABOUT YOU!
UH, REALLY?
AH! YOU'RE FINALLY HERE! QUICK! QUICK! HURRY! HURRY!
OOOH! IT'S SO BEAUTIFUL!
YOU'RE GOING TO MEET OBERON AND TITIANA, THE KING AND QUEEN OF THE FAIRIES!
IT'S A GREAT PRIVILEGE THAT VERY FEW HUMANS HAVE EVER HAD!

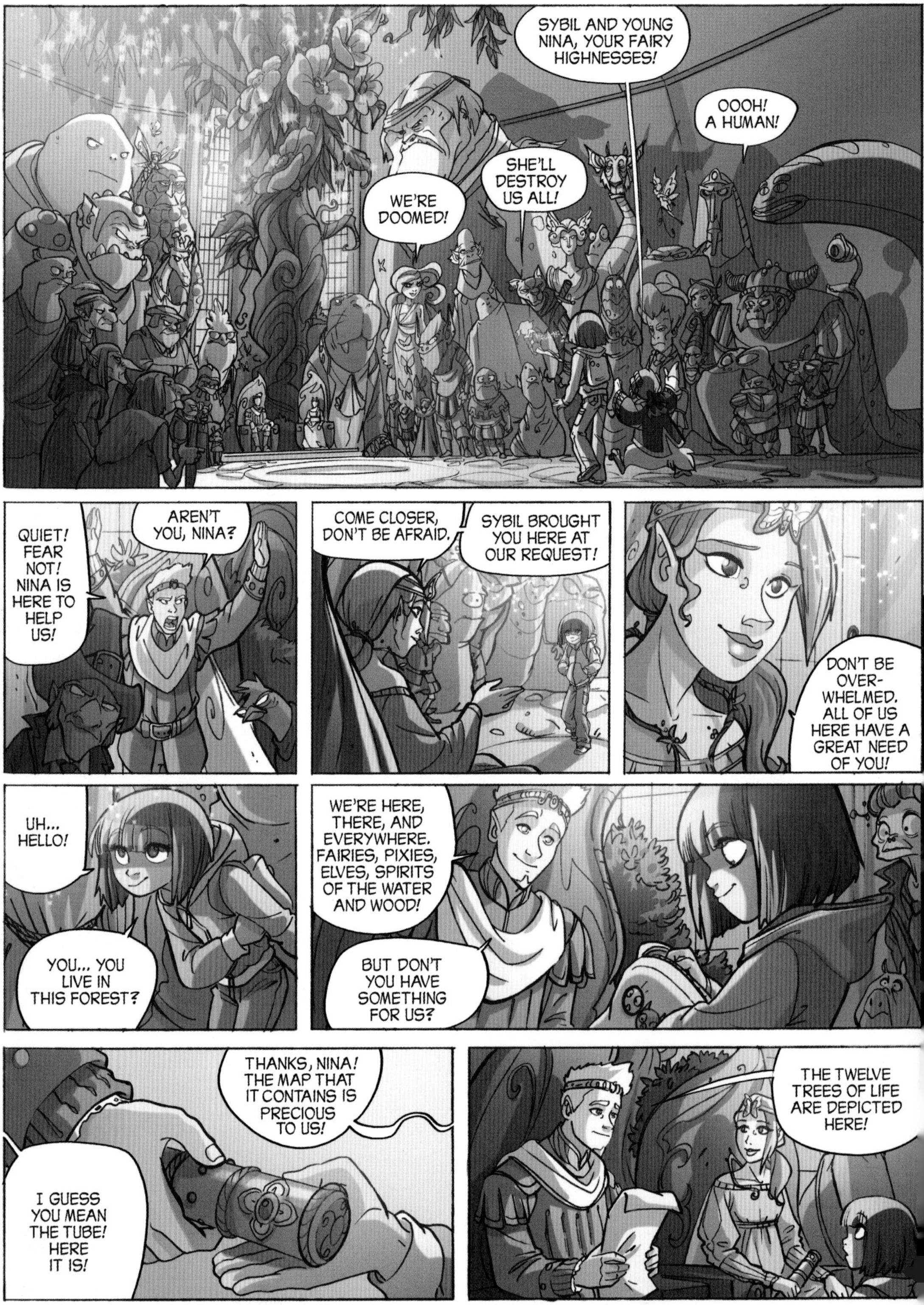
SYBIL AND YOUNG NINA, YOUR FAIRY HIGHNESSES!
OOOH! A HUMAN!
SHE'LL DESTROY US ALL!
WE'RE DOOMED!
QUIET! FEAR NOT! NINA IS HERE TO HELP US!
AREN'T YOU, NINA?
COME CLOSER, DON'T BE AFRAID.
SYBIL BROUGHT YOU HERE AT OUR REQUEST!
DON'T BE OVER-WHELMED. ALL OF US HERE HAVE A GREAT NEED OF YOU!
UH... HELLO!
YOU... YOU LIVE IN THIS FOREST?
WE'RE HERE, THERE, AND EVERYWHERE. FAIRIES, PIXIES, ELVES, SPIRITS OF THE WATER AND WOOD!
BUT DON'T YOU HAVE SOMETHING FOR US?
I GUESS YOU MEAN THE TUBE! HERE IT IS!
THANKS, NINA! THE MAP THAT IT CONTAINS IS PRECIOUS TO US!
THE TWELVE TREES OF LIFE ARE DEPICTED HERE!

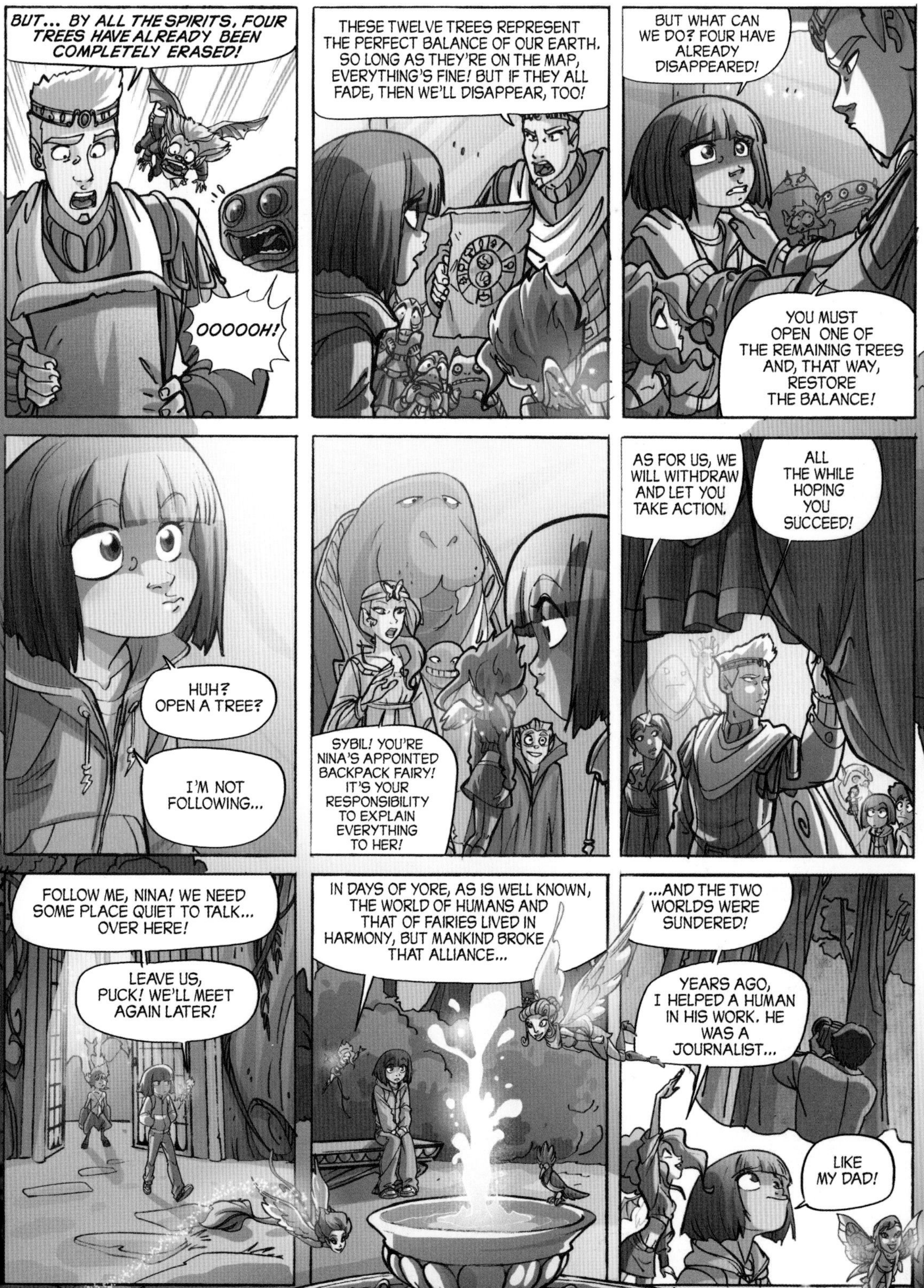

BUT... BY ALL THE SPIRITS, FOUR TREES HAVE ALREADY BEEN COMPLETELY ERASED!
OOOOOH!
THESE TWELVE TREES REPRESENT THE PERFECT BALANCE OF OUR EARTH. SO LONG AS THEY'RE ON THE MAP, EVERYTHING'S FINE! BUT IF THEY ALL FADE, THEN WE'LL DISAPPEAR, TOO!
BUT WHAT CAN WE DO? FOUR HAVE ALREADY DISAPPEARED!
YOU MUST OPEN ONE OF THE REMAINING TREES AND, THAT WAY, RESTORE THE BALANCE!
HUH? OPEN A TREE?
I'M NOT FOLLOWING...
SYBIL! YOU'RE NINA'S APPOINTED BACKPACK FAIRY! IT'S YOUR RESPONSIBILITY TO EXPLAIN EVERYTHING TO HER!
AS FOR US, WE WILL WITHDRAW AND LET YOU TAKE ACTION.
ALL THE WHILE HOPING YOU SUCCEED!
FOLLOW ME, NINA! WE NEED SOME PLACE QUIET TO TALK... OVER HERE!
LEAVE US, PUCK! WE'LL MEET AGAIN LATER!
IN DAYS OF YORE, AS IS WELL KNOWN, THE WORLD OF HUMANS AND THAT OF FAIRIES LIVED IN HARMONY, BUT MANKIND BROKE THAT ALLIANCE...
...AND THE TWO WORLDS WERE SUNDERED!
YEARS AGO, I HELPED A HUMAN IN HIS WORK. HE WAS A JOURNALIST...
LIKE MY DAD!

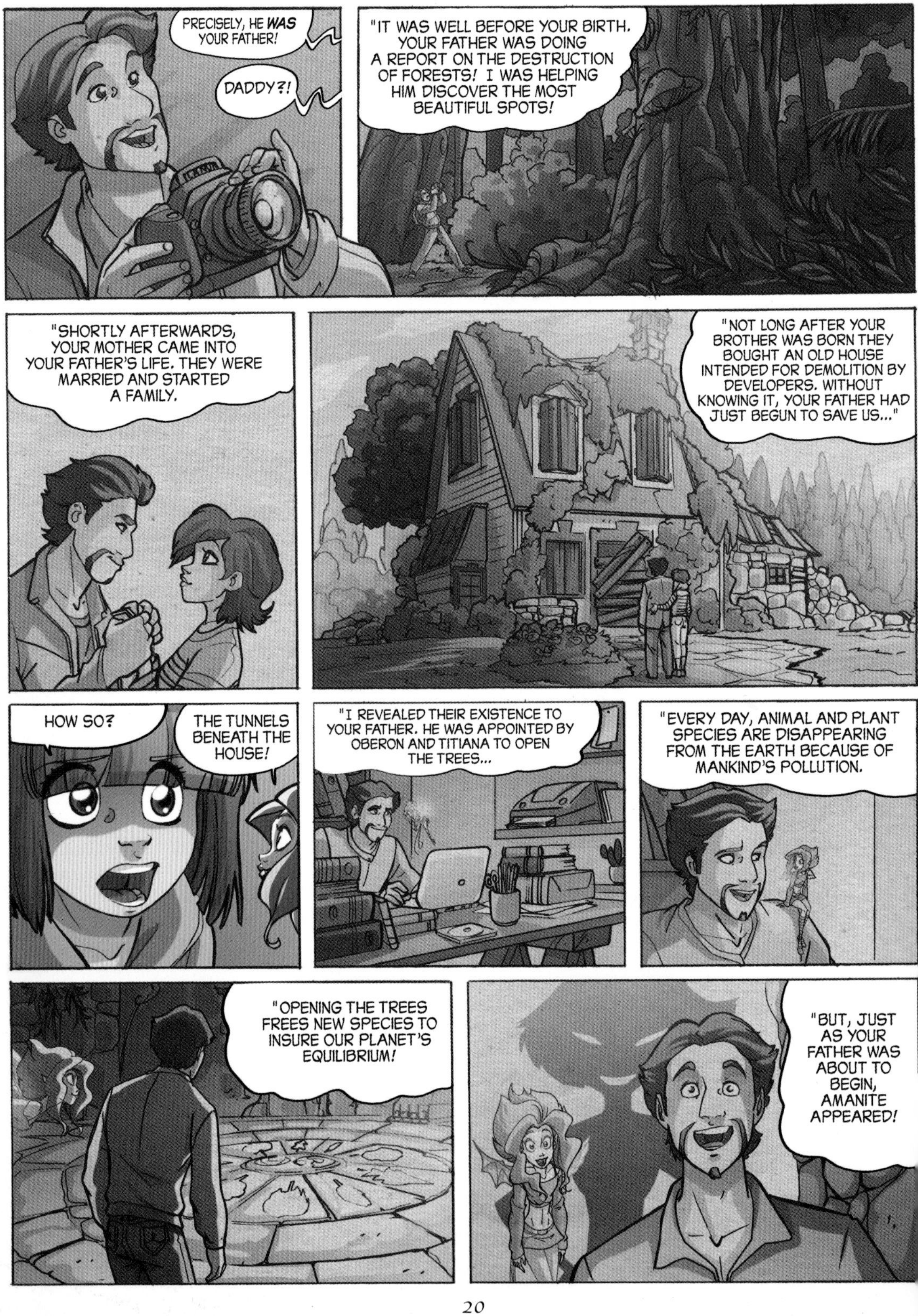
PRECISELY, HE WAS YOUR FATHER!
DADDY?!
"IT WAS WELL BEFORE YOUR BIRTH. YOUR FATHER WAS DOING A REPORT ON THE DESTRUCTION OF FORESTS! I WAS HELPING HIM DISCOVER THE MOST BEAUTIFUL SPOTS!
"SHORTLY AFTERWARDS, YOUR MOTHER CAME INTO YOUR FATHER'S LIFE. THEY WERE MARRIED AND STARTED A FAMILY.
"NOT LONG AFTER YOUR BROTHER WAS BORN THEY BOUGHT AN OLD HOUSE INTENDED FOR DEMOLITION BY DEVELOPERS. WITHOUT KNOWING IT, YOUR FATHER HAD JUST BEGUN TO SAVE US..."
HOW SO?
THE TUNNELS BENEATH THE HOUSE!
"I REVEALED THEIR EXISTENCE TO YOUR FATHER. HE WAS APPOINTED BY OBERON AND TITIANA TO OPEN THE TREES...
"EVERY DAY, ANIMAL AND PLANT SPECIES ARE DISAPPEARING FROM THE EARTH BECAUSE OF MANKIND'S POLLUTION.
"OPENING THE TREES FREES NEW SPECIES TO INSURE OUR PLANET'S EQUILIBRIUM!
"BUT, JUST AS YOUR FATHER WAS ABOUT TO BEGIN, AMANITE APPEARED!

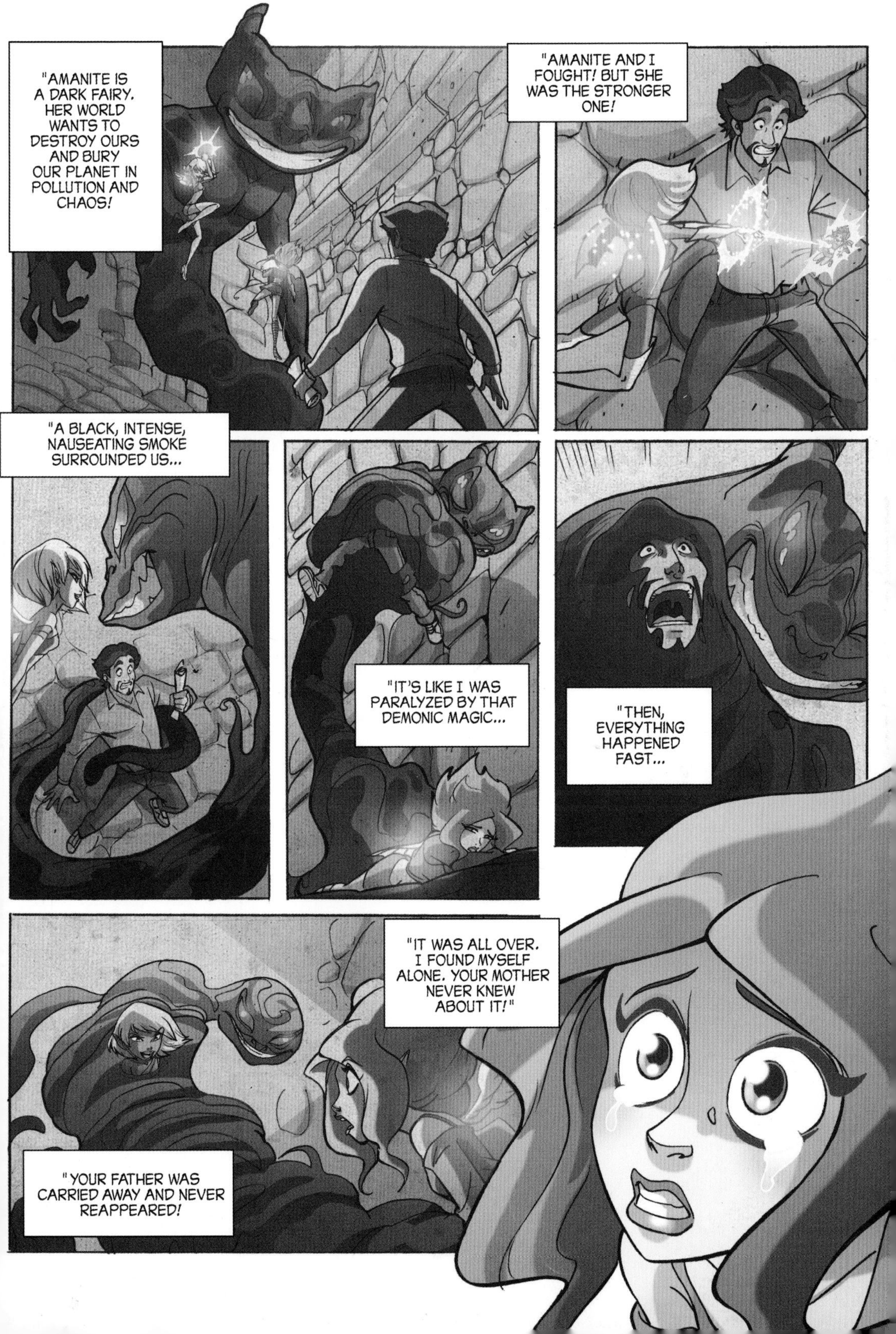
"AMANITE IS A DARK FAIRY. HER WORLD WANTS TO DESTROY OURS AND BURY OUR PLANET IN POLLUTION AND CHAOS!
"AMANITE AND I FOUGHT! BUT SHE WAS THE STRONGER ONE!
"A BLACK, INTENSE, NAUSEATING SMOKE SURROUNDED US...
"IT'S LIKE I WAS PARALYZED BY THAT DEMONIC MAGIC...
"THEN, EVERYTHING HAPPENED FAST...
"IT WAS ALL OVER. I FOUND MYSELF ALONE. YOUR MOTHER NEVER KNEW ABOUT IT!"
"YOUR FATHER WAS CARRIED AWAY AND NEVER REAPPEARED!

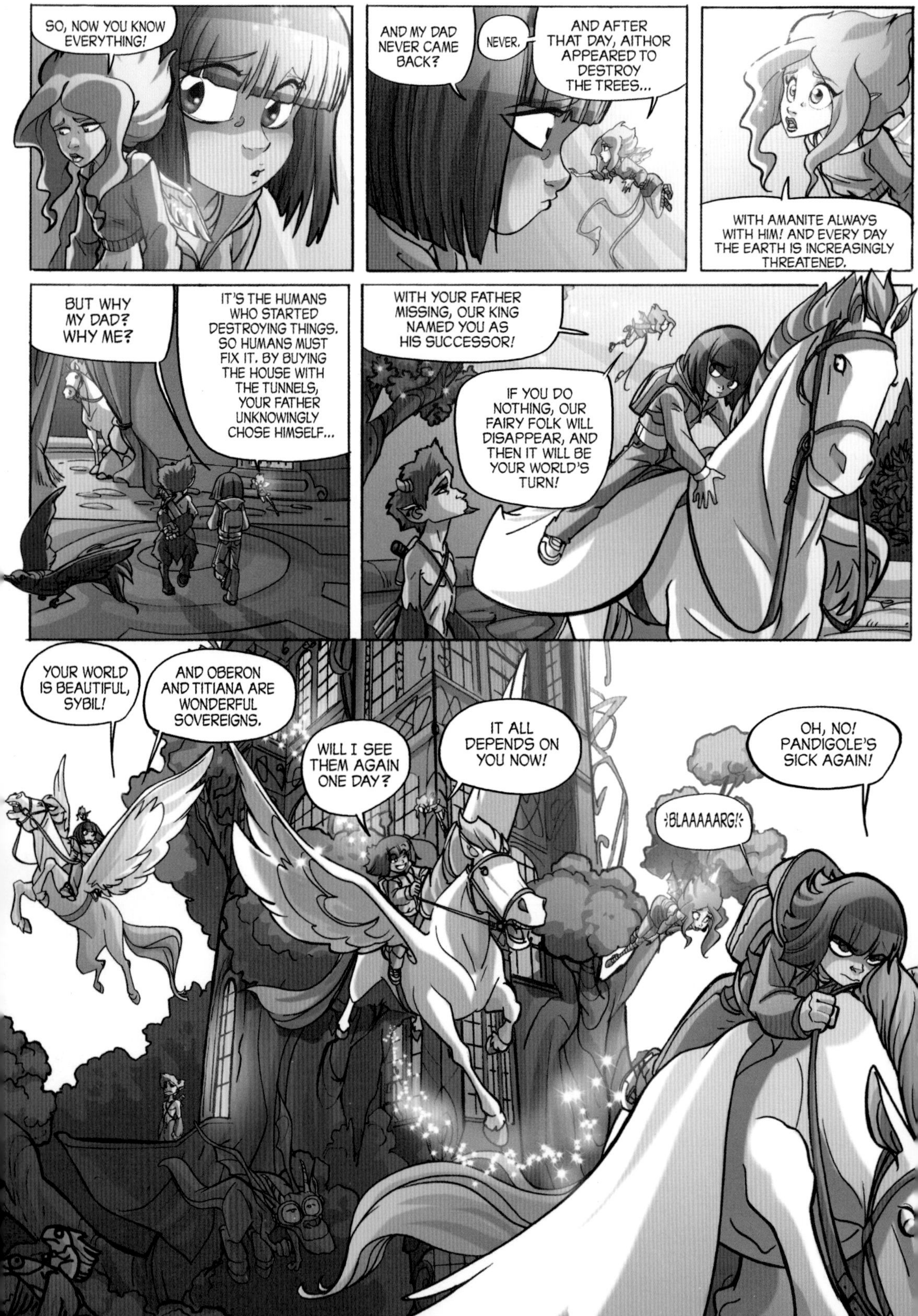
SO, NOW YOU KNOW EVERYTHING!
AND MY DAD NEVER CAME BACK?
NEVER.
AND AFTER THAT DAY, AITHOR APPEARED TO DESTROY THE TREES...
WITH AMANITE ALWAYS WITH HIM! AND EVERY DAY THE EARTH IS INCREASINGLY THREATENED.
BUT WHY MY DAD? WHY ME?
IT'S THE HUMANS WHO STARTED DESTROYING THINGS. SO HUMANS MUST FIX IT. BY BUYING THE HOUSE WITH THE TUNNELS, YOUR FATHER UNKNOWINGLY CHOSE HIMSELF...
WITH YOUR FATHER MISSING, OUR KING NAMED YOU AS HIS SUCCESSOR!
IF YOU DO NOTHING, OUR FAIRY FOLK WILL DISAPPEAR, AND THEN IT WILL BE YOUR WORLD'S TURN!
YOUR WORLD IS BEAUTIFUL, SYBIL!
AND OBERON AND TITIANA ARE WONDERFUL SOVEREIGNS.
WILL I SEE THEM AGAIN ONE DAY?
IT ALL DEPENDS ON YOU NOW!
OH, NO! PANDIGOLE'S SICK AGAIN!
BLAAAAARG!

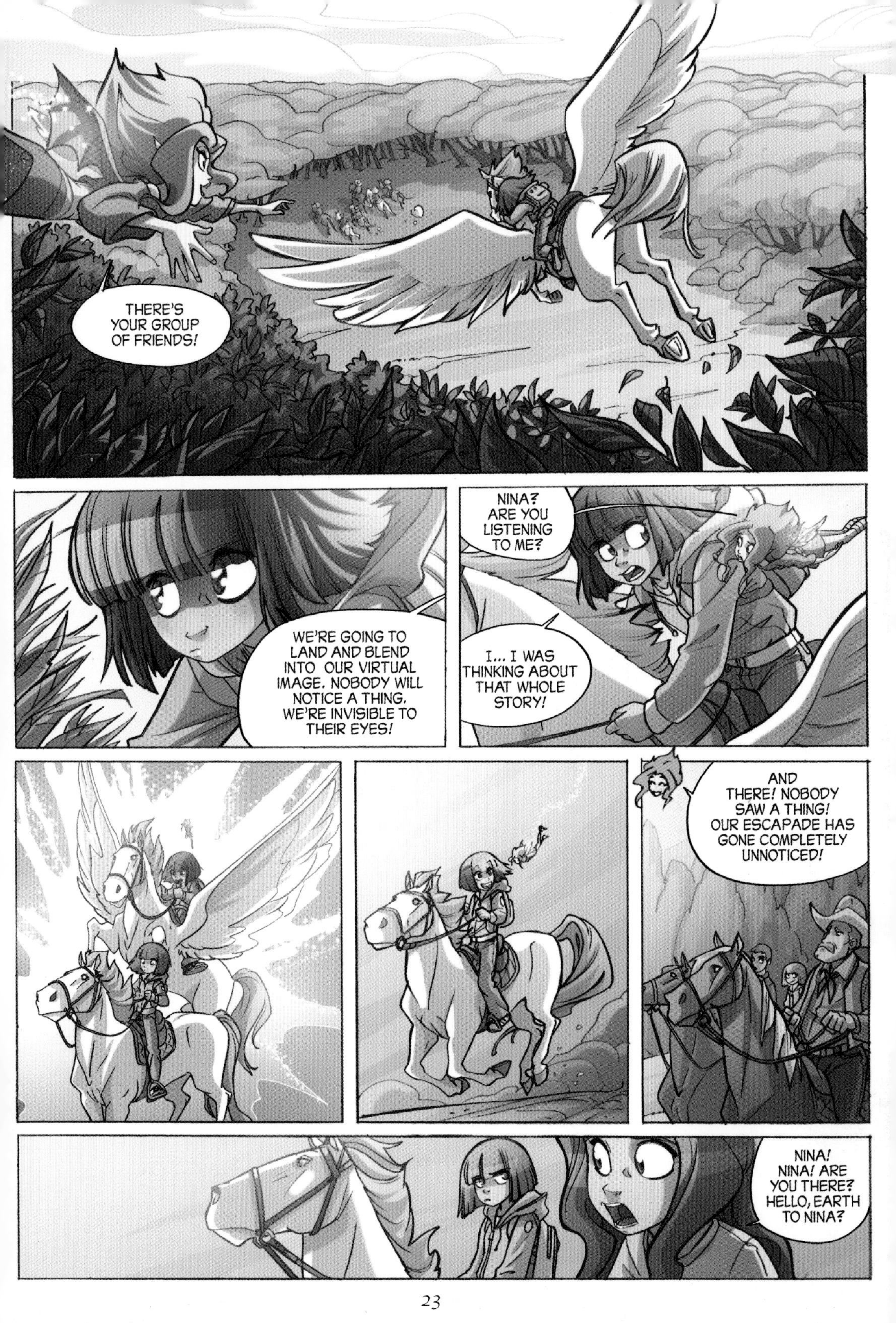
THERE'S YOUR GROUP OF FRIENDS!
WE'RE GOING TO LAND AND BLEND INTO OUR VIRTUAL IMAGE. NOBODY WILL NOTICE A THING. WE'RE INVISIBLE TO THEIR EYES!
NINA? ARE YOU LISTENING TO ME?
I... I WAS THINKING ABOUT THAT WHOLE STORY!
AND THERE! NOBODY SAW A THING! OUR ESCAPADE HAS GONE COMPLETELY UNNOTICED!
NINA! NINA! ARE YOU THERE? HELLO, EARTH TO NINA?

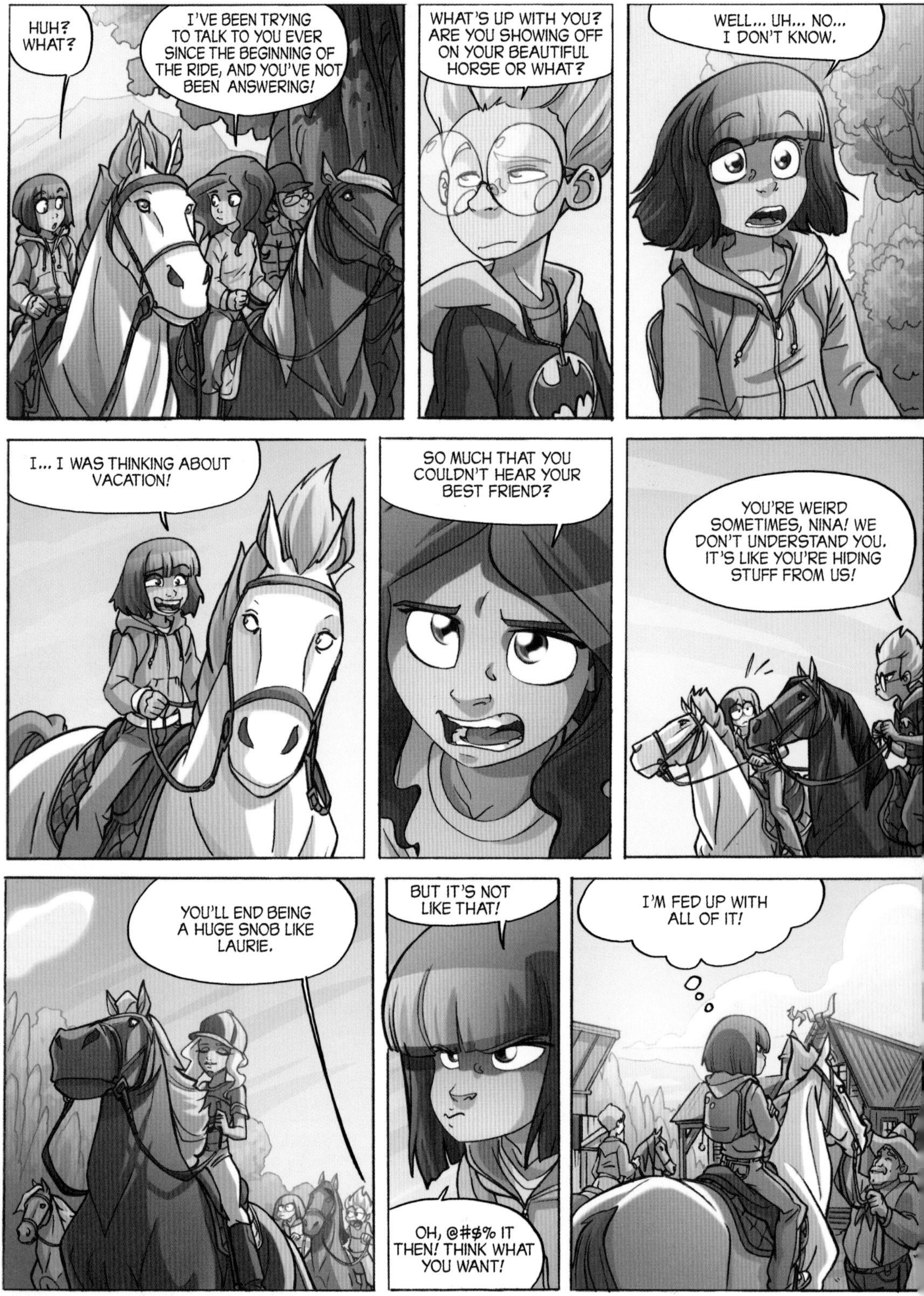
HUH? WHAT?
I'VE BEEN TRYING TO TALK TO YOU EVER SINCE THE BEGINNING OF THE RIDE, AND YOU'VE NOT BEEN ANSWERING!
WHAT'S UP WITH YOU? ARE YOU SHOWING OFF ON YOUR BEAUTIFUL HORSE OR WHAT?
WELL... UH... NO... I DON'T KNOW.
I... I WAS THINKING ABOUT VACATION!
SO MUCH THAT YOU COULDN'T HEAR YOUR BEST FRIEND?
YOU'RE WEIRD SOMETIMES, NINA! WE DON'T UNDERSTAND YOU. IT'S LIKE YOU'RE HIDING STUFF FROM US!
YOU'LL END BEING A HUGE SNOB LIKE LAURIE.
BUT IT'S NOT LIKE THAT!
OH, @#$% IT THEN! THINK WHAT YOU WANT!
I'M FED UP WITH ALL OF IT!

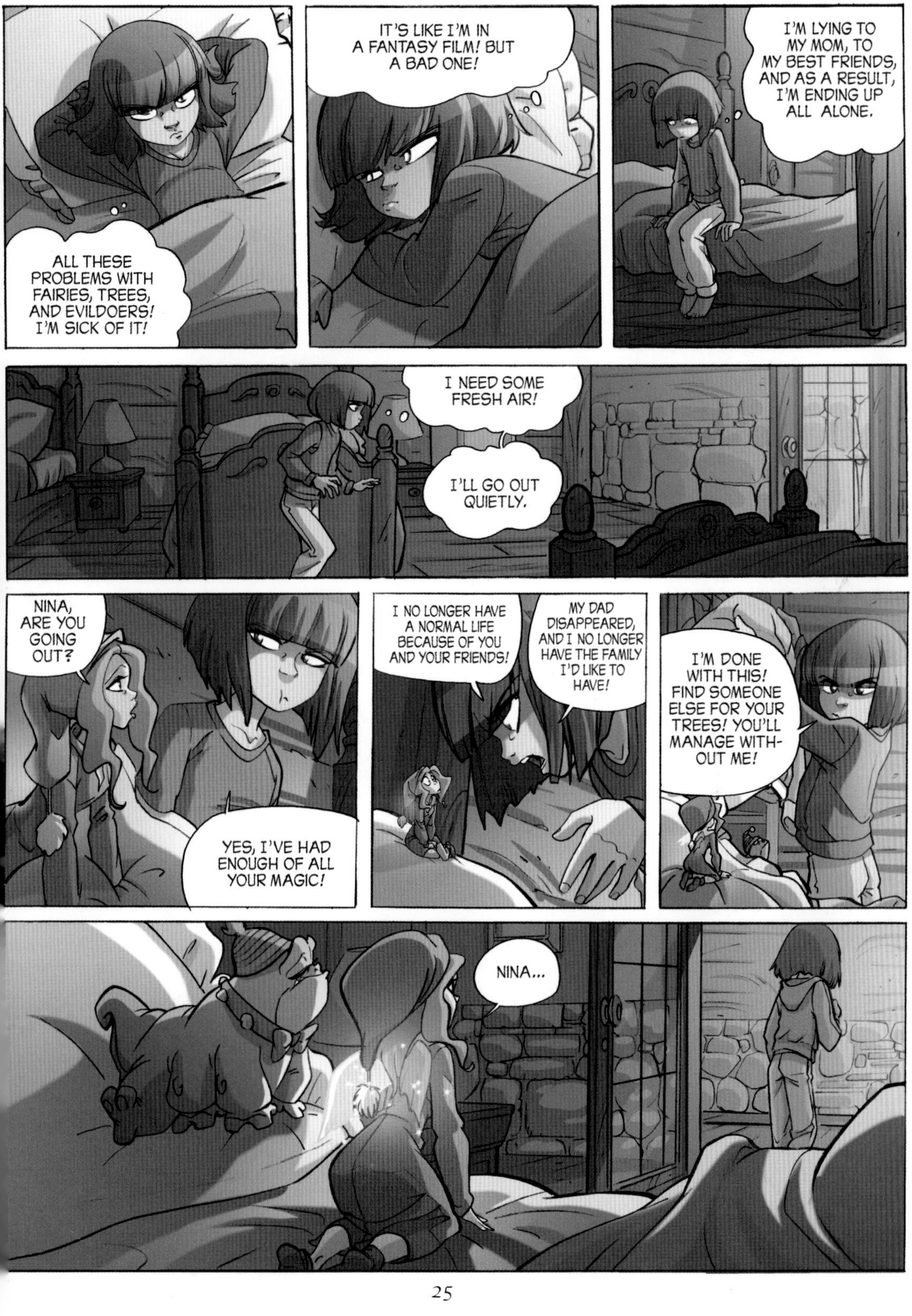
ALL THESE PROBLEMS WITH FAIRIES, TREES, AND EVILDOERS! I'M SICK OF IT!
IT'S LIKE I'M IN A FANTASY FILM! BUT A BAD ONE!
I'M LYING TO MY MOM, TO MY BEST FRIENDS, AND AS A RESULT, I'M ENDING UP ALL ALONE.
I NEED SOME FRESH AIR!
I'LL GO OUT QUIETLY.
NINA, ARE YOU GOING OUT?
YES, I'VE HAD ENOUGH OF ALL YOUR MAGIC!
I NO LONGER HAVE A NORMAL LIFE BECAUSE OF YOU AND YOUR FRIENDS!
MY DAD DISAPPEARED, AND I NO LONGER HAVE THE FAMILY I'D LIKE TO HAVE!
I'M DONE WITH THIS! FIND SOMEONE ELSE FOR YOUR TREES! YOU'LL MANAGE WITH-OUT ME!
NINA...

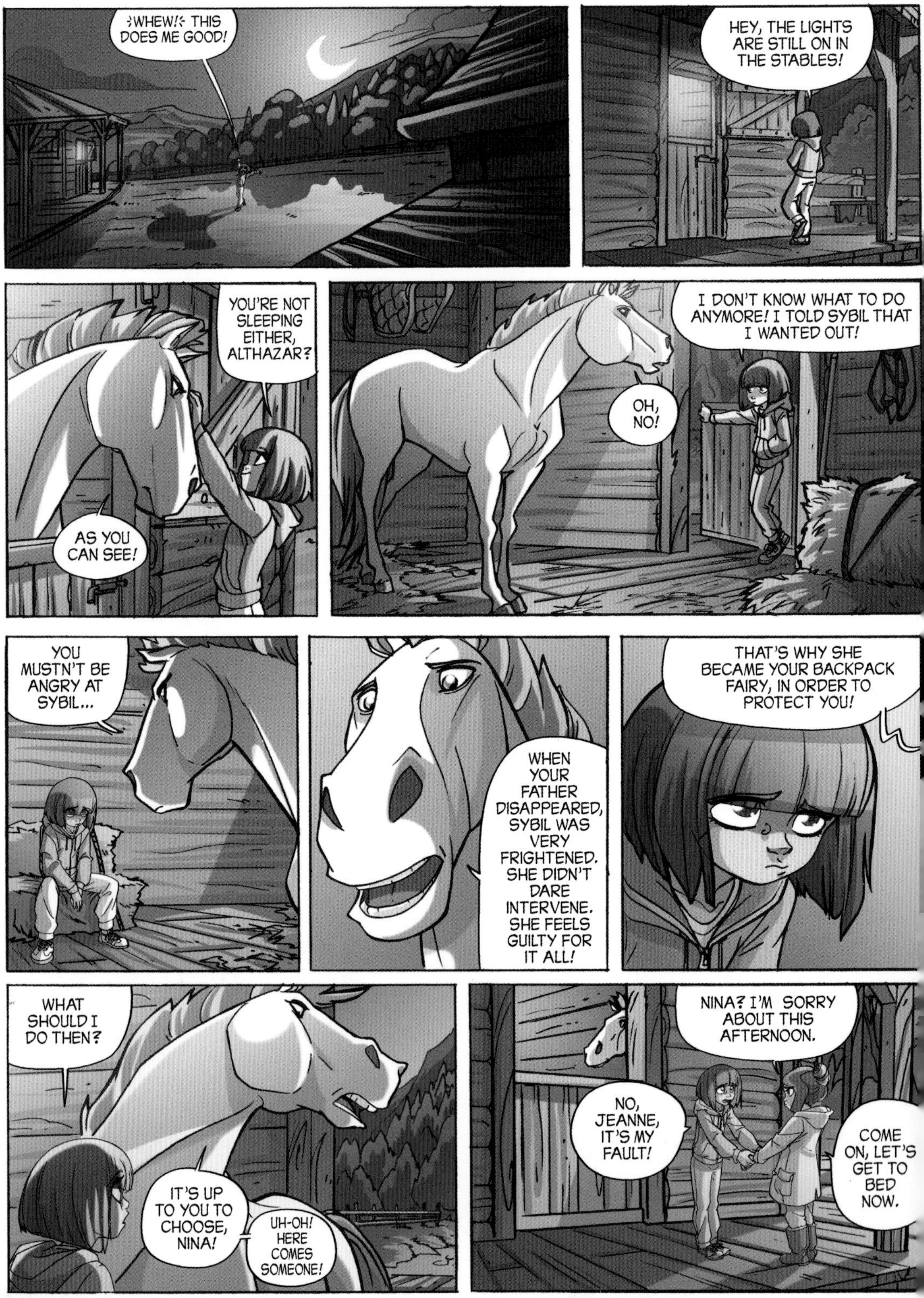

WHEW! THIS DOES ME GOOD!
HEY, THE LIGHTS ARE STILL ON IN THE STABLES!
YOU'RE NOT SLEEPING EITHER, ALTHAZAR?
AS YOU CAN SEE!
I DON'T KNOW WHAT TO DO ANYMORE! I TOLD SYBIL THAT I WANTED OUT!
OH, NO!
YOU MUSTN'T BE ANGRY AT SYBIL...
WHEN YOUR FATHER DISAPPEARED, SYBIL WAS VERY FRIGHTENED. SHE DIDN'T DARE INTERVENE. SHE FEELS GUILTY FOR IT ALL!
THAT'S WHY SHE BECAME YOUR BACKPACK FAIRY, IN ORDER TO PROTECT YOU!
WHAT SHOULD I DO THEN?
IT'S UP TO YOU TO CHOOSE, NINA!
UH-OH! HERE COMES SOMEONE!
NINA? I'M SORRY ABOUT THIS AFTERNOON.
NO, JEANNE, IT'S MY FAULT!
COME ON, LET'S GET TO BED NOW.

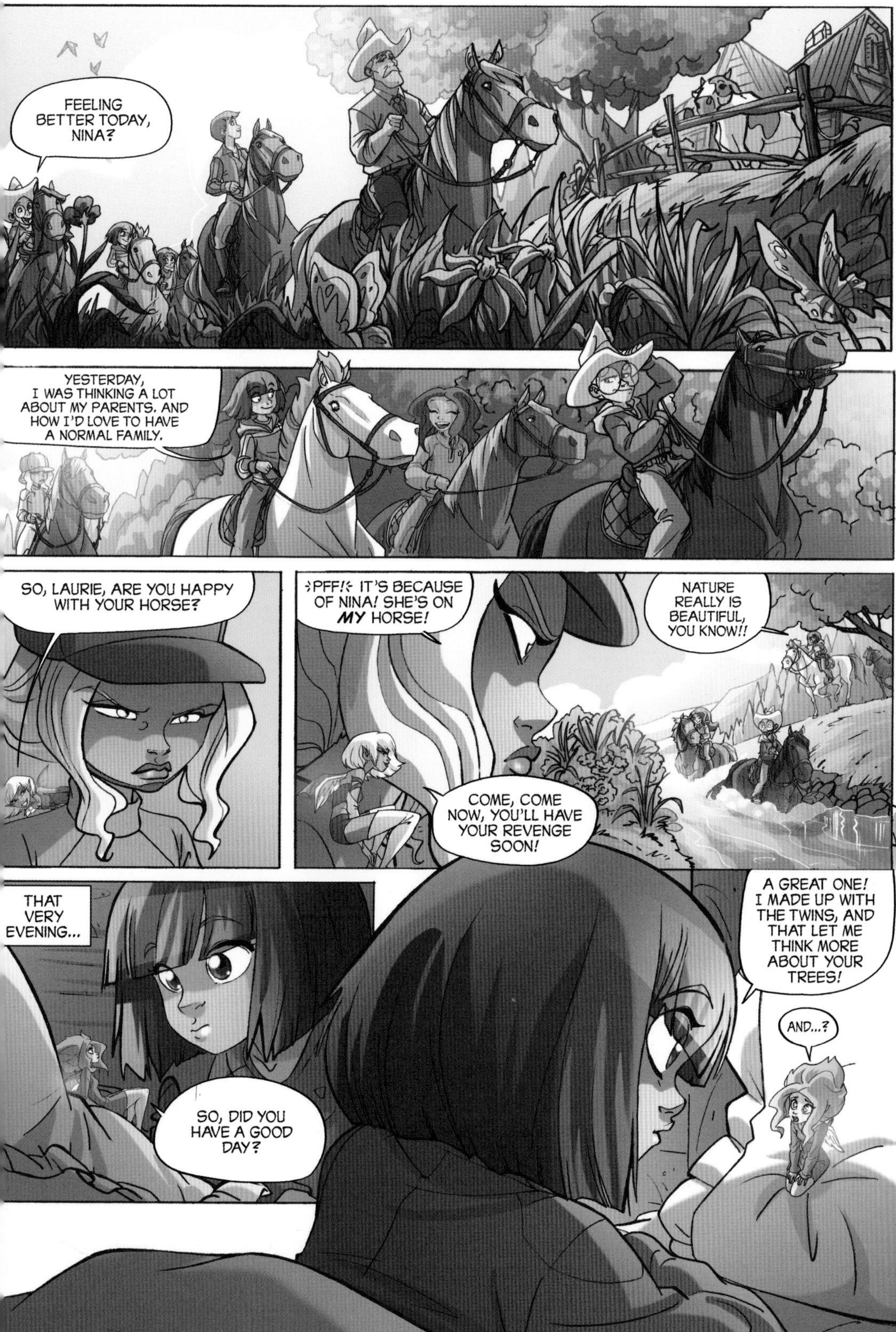

FEELING BETTER TODAY, NINA?
YESTERDAY, I WAS THINKING A LOT ABOUT MY PARENTS. AND HOW I'D LOVE TO HAVE A NORMAL FAMILY.
SO, LAURIE, ARE YOU HAPPY WITH YOUR HORSE?
PFF! IT'S BECAUSE OF NINA! SHE'S ON MY HORSE!
NATURE REALLY IS BEAUTIFUL, YOU KNOW!!
COME, COME NOW, YOU'LL HAVE YOUR REVENGE SOON!
THAT VERY EVENING...
SO, DID YOU HAVE A GOOD DAY?
A GREAT ONE! I MADE UP WITH THE TWINS, AND THAT LET ME THINK MORE ABOUT YOUR TREES!
AND...?

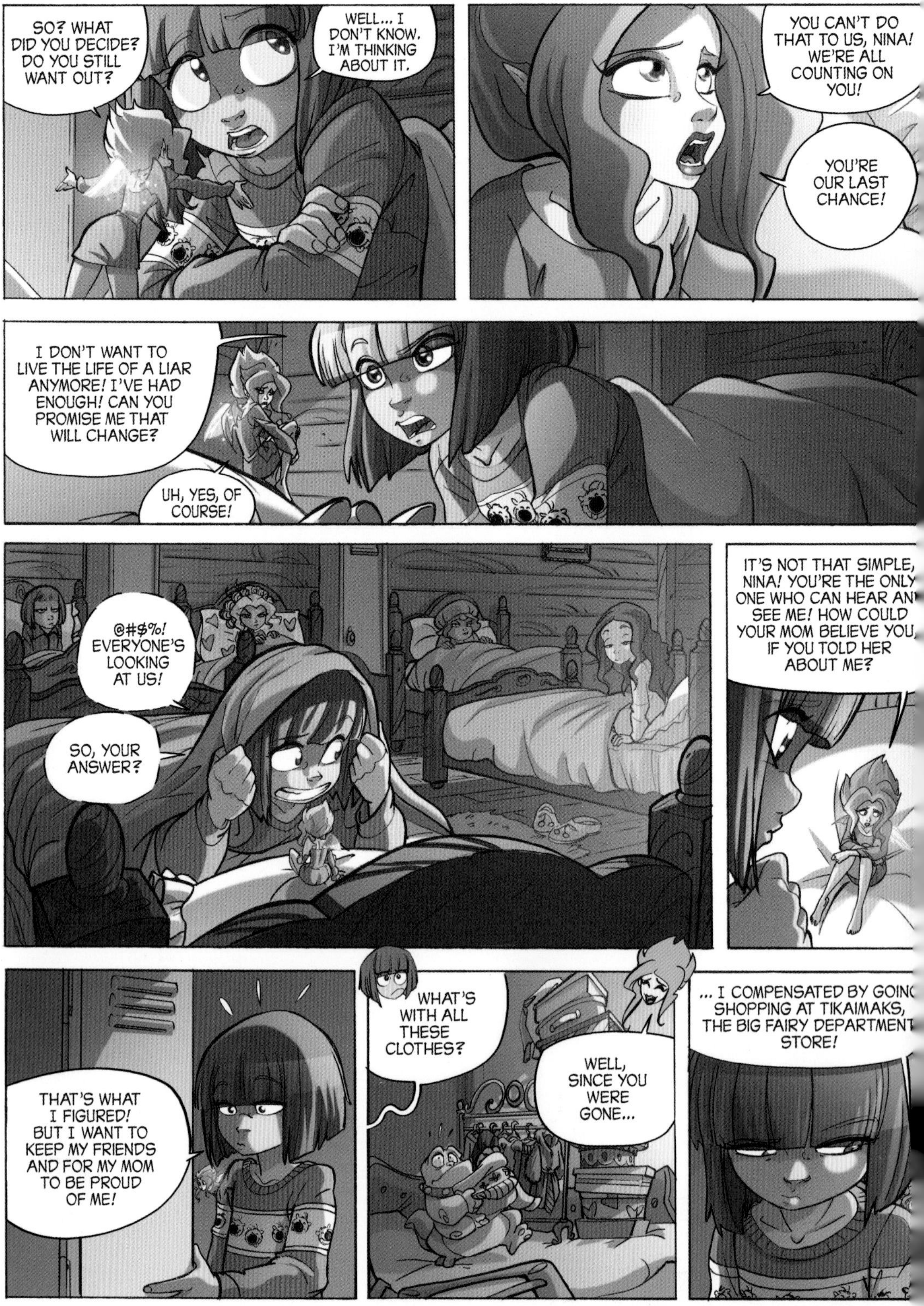
SO? WHAT DID YOU DECIDE? DO YOU STILL WANT OUT?
WELL... I DON'T KNOW. I'M THINKING ABOUT IT.
YOU CAN'T DO THAT TO US, NINA! WE'RE ALL COUNTING ON YOU!
YOU'RE OUR LAST CHANCE!
I DON'T WANT TO LIVE THE LIFE OF A LIAR ANYMORE! I'VE HAD ENOUGH! CAN YOU PROMISE ME THAT WILL CHANGE?
UH, YES, OF COURSE!
@#$%! EVERYONE'S LOOKING AT US!
SO, YOUR ANSWER?
IT'S NOT THAT SIMPLE, NINA! YOU'RE THE ONLY ONE WHO CAN HEAR AN SEE ME! HOW COULD YOUR MOM BELIEVE YOU, IF YOU TOLD HER ABOUT ME?
THAT'S WHAT I FIGURED! BUT I WANT TO KEEP MY FRIENDS AND FOR MY MOM TO BE PROUD OF ME!
WHAT'S WITH ALL THESE CLOTHES?
WELL, SINCE YOU WERE GONE...
... I COMPENSATED BY GOIN SHOPPING AT TIKAIMAKS, THE BIG FAIRY DEPARTMENT STORE!

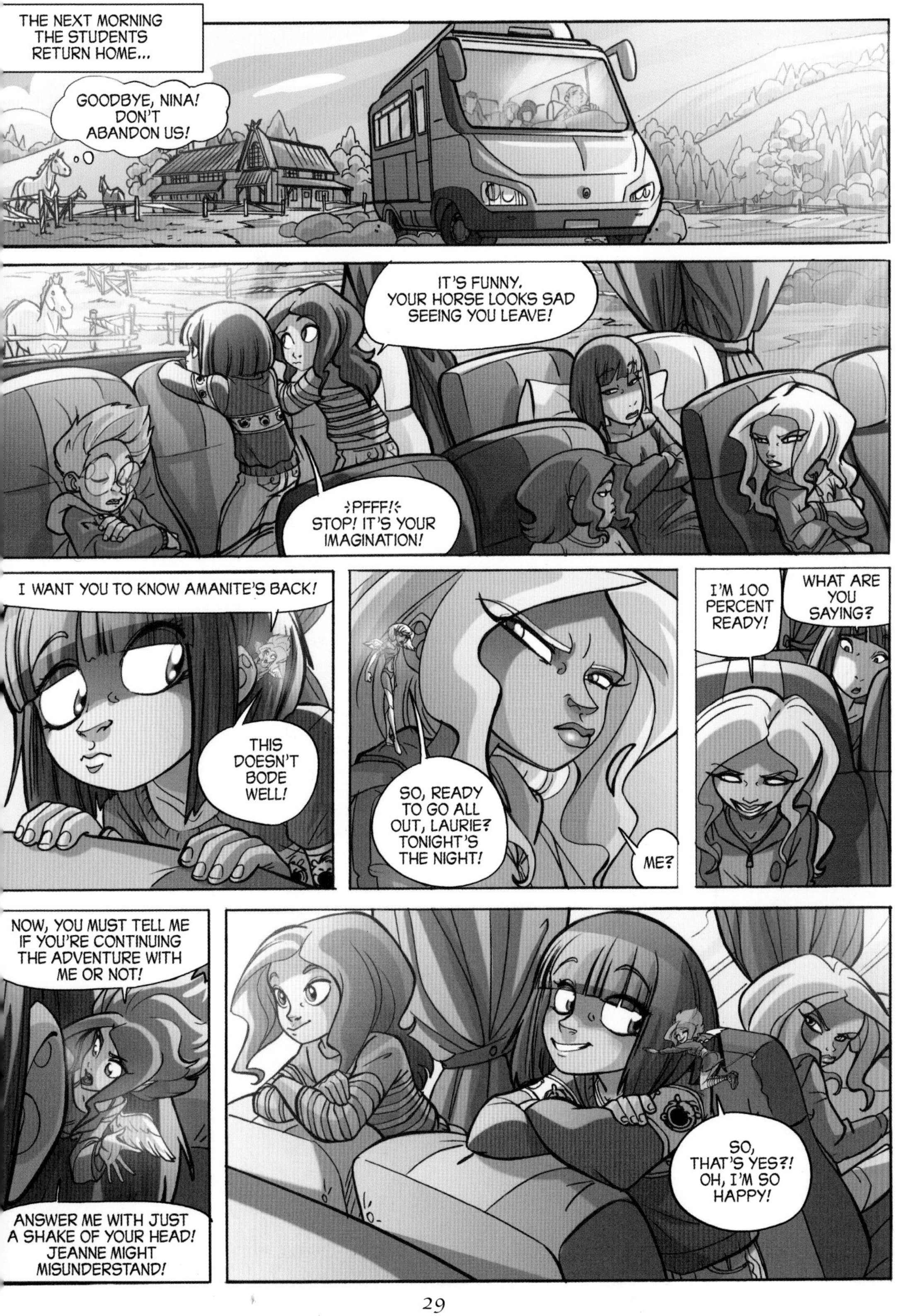
THE NEXT MORNING THE STUDENTS RETURN HOME...
GOODBYE, NINA! DON'T ABANDON US!
IT'S FUNNY. YOUR HORSE LOOKS SAD SEEING YOU LEAVE!
PFFF! STOP! IT'S YOUR IMAGINATION!
I WANT YOU TO KNOW AMANITE'S BACK!
THIS DOESN'T BODE WELL!
SO, READY TO GO ALL OUT, LAURIE? TONIGHT'S THE NIGHT!
ME?
I'M 100 PERCENT READY!
WHAT ARE YOU SAYING?
NOW, YOU MUST TELL ME IF YOU'RE CONTINUING THE ADVENTURE WITH ME OR NOT!
ANSWER ME WITH JUST A SHAKE OF YOUR HEAD! JEANNE MIGHT MISUNDERSTAND!
SO, THAT'S YES?! OH, I'M SO HAPPY!

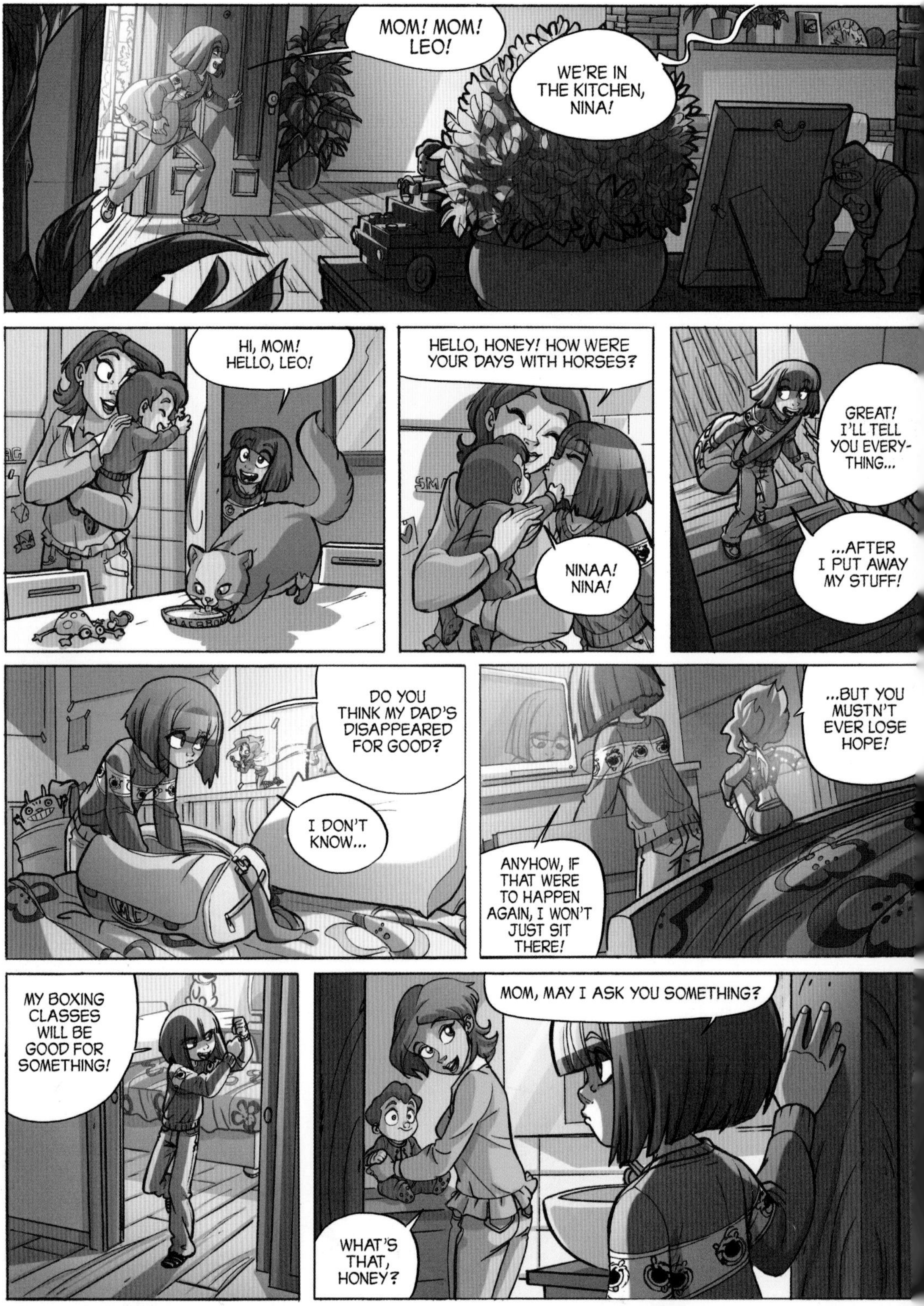
MOM! MOM! LEO!
WE'RE IN THE KITCHEN, NINA!
HI, MOM! HELLO, LEO!
HELLO, HONEY! HOW WERE YOUR DAYS WITH HORSES?
NINAA! NINA!
GREAT! I'LL TELL YOU EVERY-THING...
...AFTER I PUT AWAY MY STUFF!
DO YOU THINK MY DAD'S DISAPPEARED FOR GOOD?
I DON'T KNOW...
...BUT YOU MUSTN'T EVER LOSE HOPE!
ANYHOW, IF THAT WERE TO HAPPEN AGAIN, I WON'T JUST SIT THERE!
MY BOXING CLASSES WILL BE GOOD FOR SOMETHING!
MOM, MAY I ASK YOU SOMETHING?
WHAT'S THAT, HONEY?

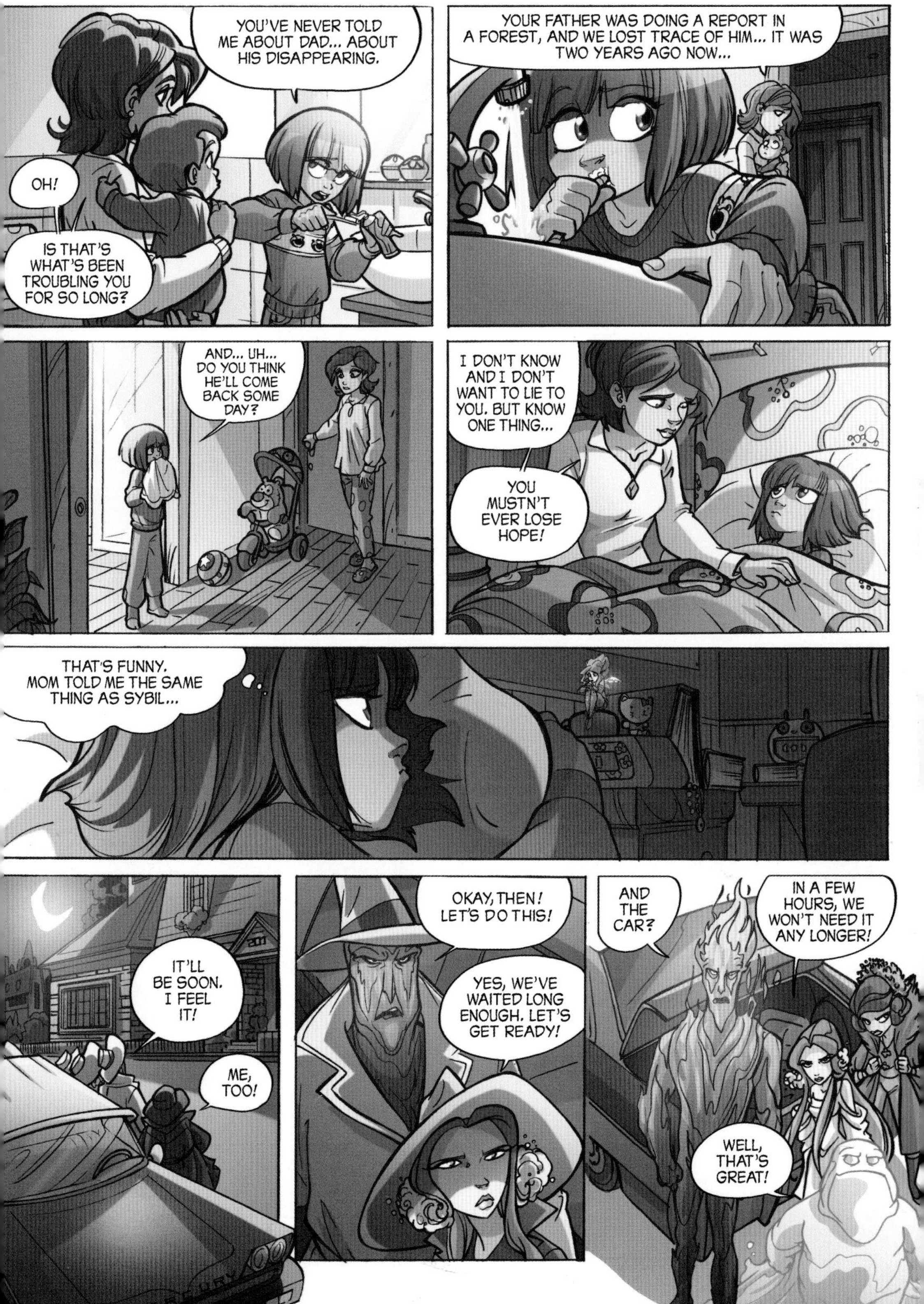
YOU'VE NEVER TOLD ME ABOUT DAD... ABOUT HIS DISAPPEARING.
OH!
IS THAT'S WHAT'S BEEN TROUBLING YOU FOR SO LONG?
YOUR FATHER WAS DOING A REPORT IN A FOREST, AND WE LOST TRACE OF HIM... IT WAS TWO YEARS AGO NOW...
AND... UH... DO YOU THINK HE'LL COME BACK SOME DAY?
I DON'T KNOW AND I DON'T WANT TO LIE TO YOU. BUT KNOW ONE THING...
YOU MUSTN'T EVER LOSE HOPE!
THAT'S FUNNY. MOM TOLD ME THE SAME THING AS SYBIL...
IT'LL BE SOON. I FEEL IT!
ME, TOO!
OKAY, THEN! LET'S DO THIS!
YES, WE'VE WAITED LONG ENOUGH. LET'S GET READY!
AND THE CAR?
IN A FEW HOURS, WE WON'T NEED IT ANY LONGER!
WELL, THAT'S GREAT!

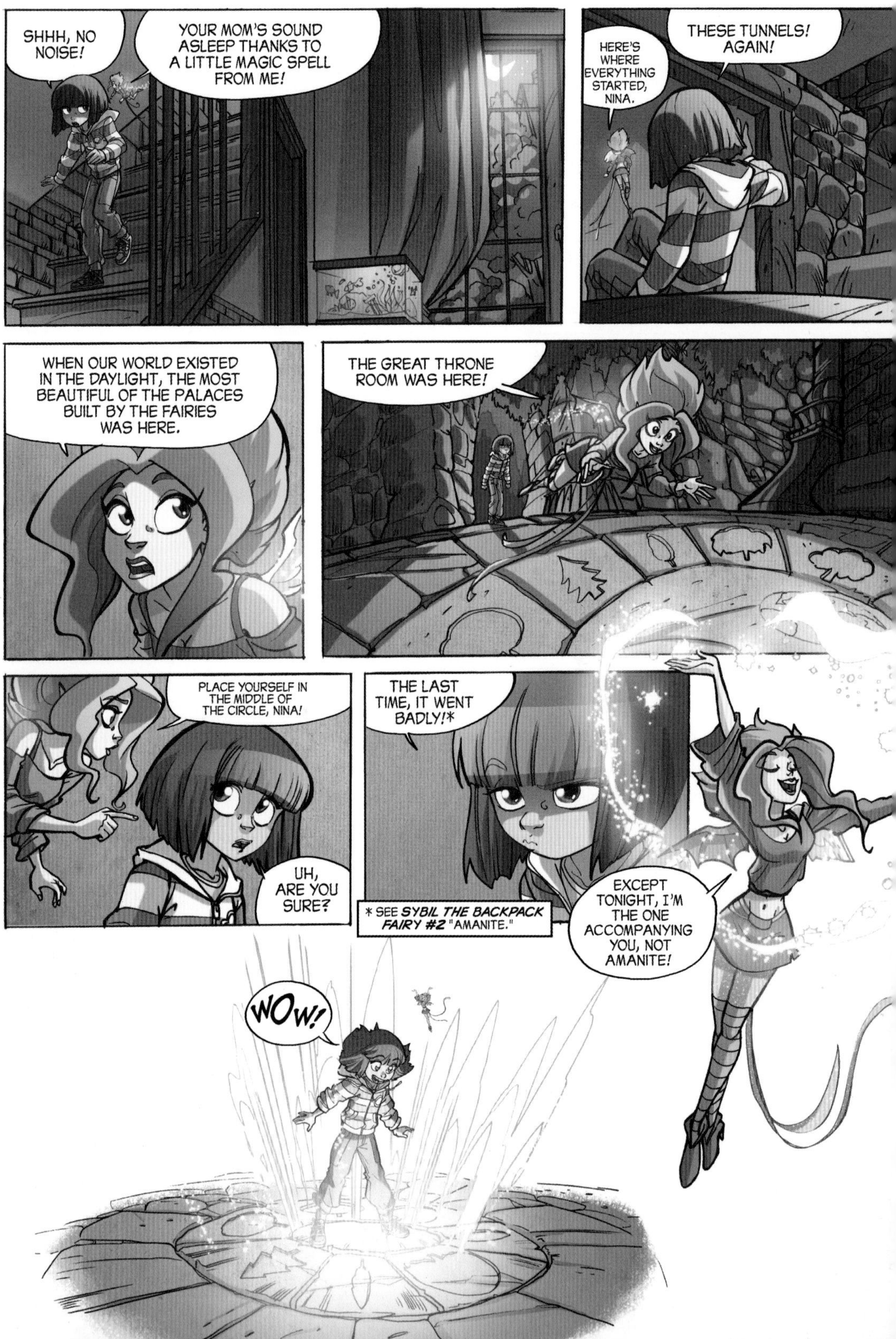

SHHH, NO NOISE!
YOUR MOM'S SOUND ASLEEP THANKS TO A LITTLE MAGIC SPELL FROM ME!
THESE TUNNELS! AGAIN!
HERE'S WHERE EVERYTHING STARTED, NINA.
WHEN OUR WORLD EXISTED IN THE DAYLIGHT, THE MOST BEAUTIFUL OF THE PALACES BUILT BY THE FAIRIES WAS HERE.
THE GREAT THRONE ROOM WAS HERE!
PLACE YOURSELF IN THE MIDDLE OF THE CIRCLE, NINA!
UH, ARE YOU SURE?
THE LAST TIME, IT WENT BADLY!*
* SEE SYBIL THE BACKPACK FAIRY #2 "AMANITE."
EXCEPT TONIGHT, I'M THE ONE ACCOMPANYING YOU, NOT AMANITE!
WOW!

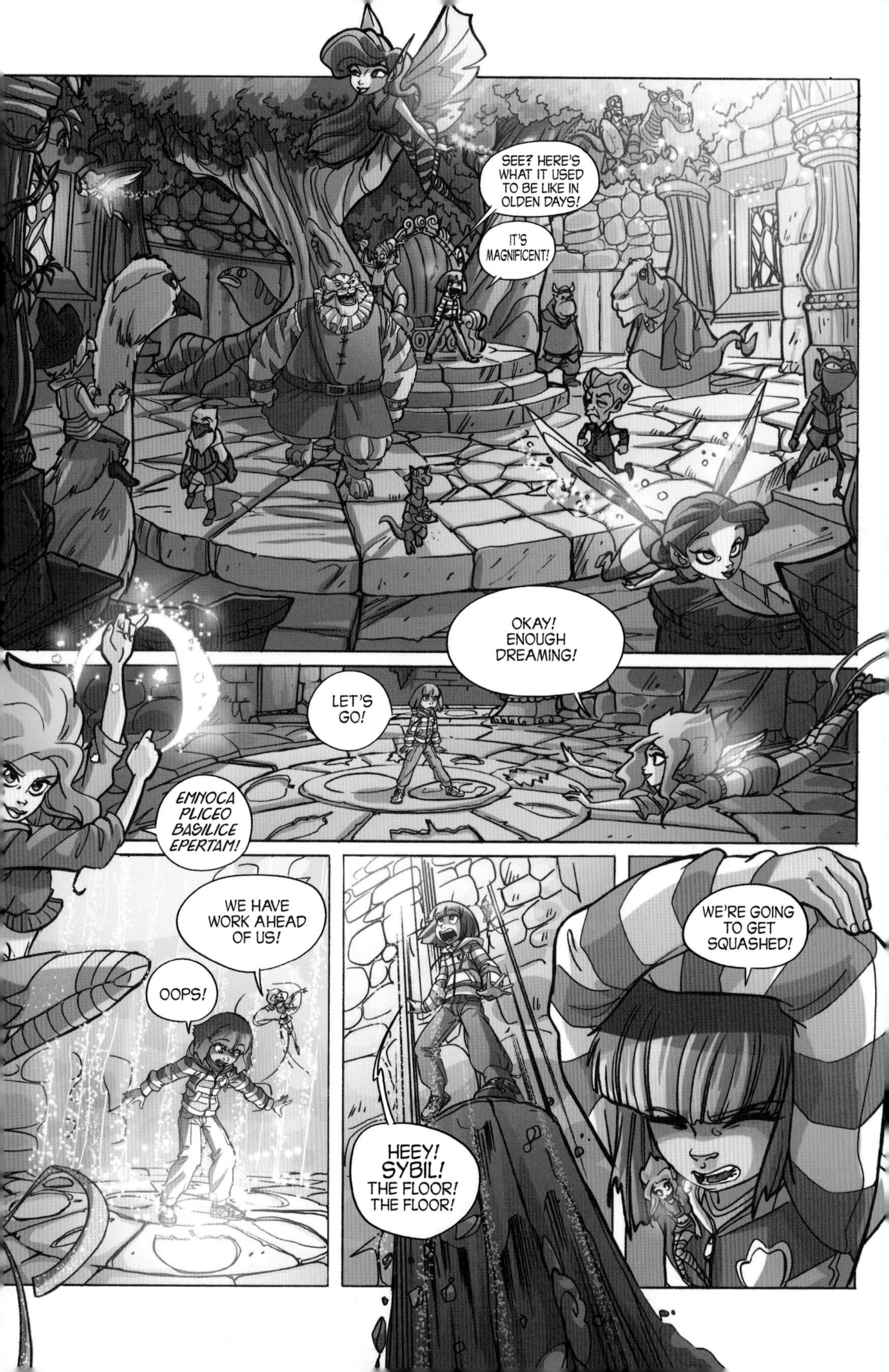
SEE? HERE'S WHAT IT USED TO BE LIKE IN OLDEN DAYS!
IT'S MAGNIFICENT!
OKAY! ENOUGH DREAMING!
LET'S GO!
EMNOCA PLICEO BASILICE EPERTAM!
WE HAVE WORK AHEAD OF US!
OOPS!
HEEY! SYBIL! THE FLOOR! THE FLOOR!
WE'RE GOING TO GET SQUASHED!

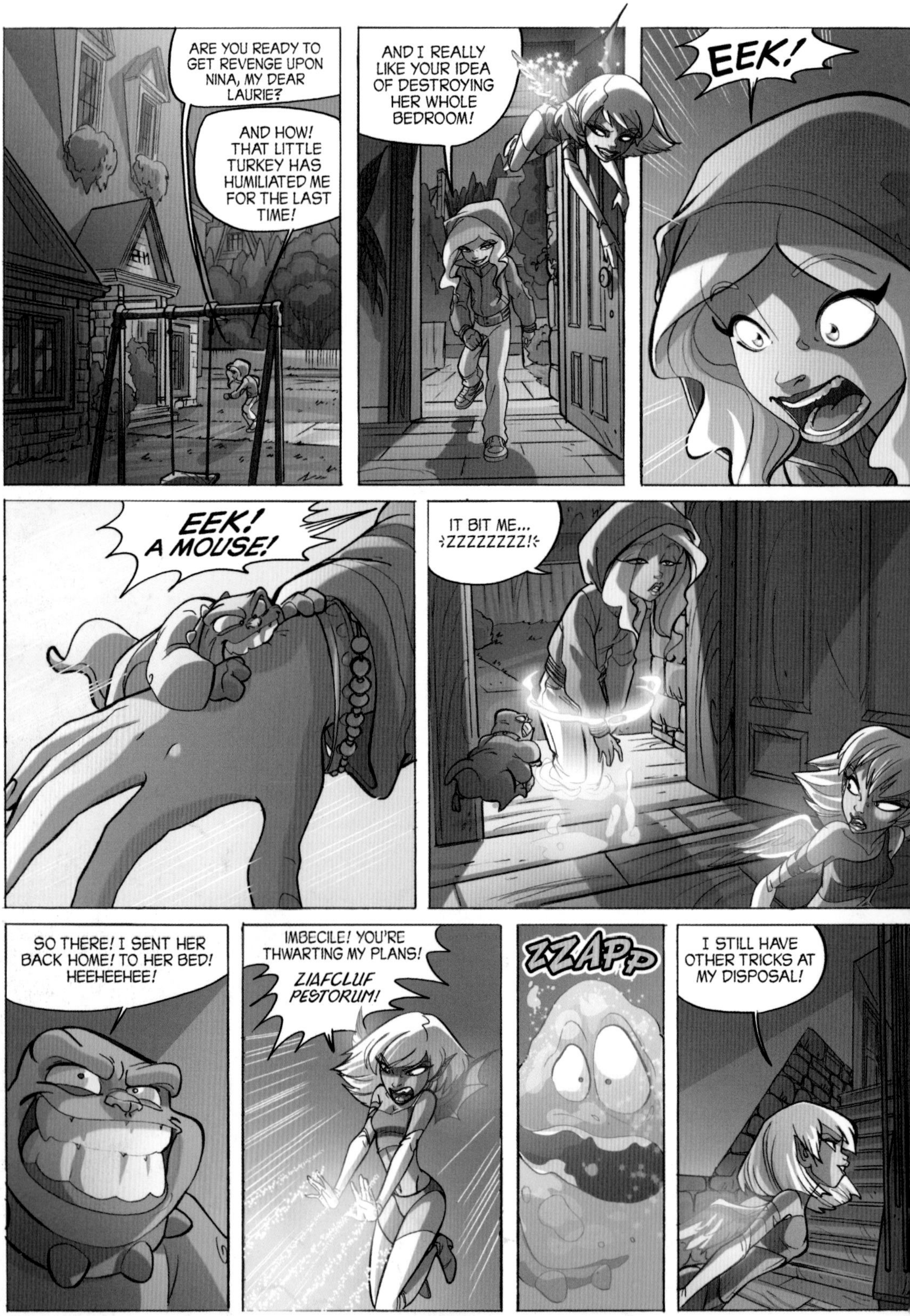
ARE YOU READY TO GET REVENGE UPON NINA, MY DEAR LAURIE?
AND HOW! THAT LITTLE TURKEY HAS HUMILIATED ME FOR THE LAST TIME!
AND I REALLY LIKE YOUR IDEA OF DESTROYING HER WHOLE BEDROOM!
EEK!
EEK! A MOUSE!
IT BIT ME... ZZZZZZZZ!
SO THERE! I SENT HER BACK HOME! TO HER BED! HEEHEEHEE!
IMBECILE! YOU'RE THWARTING MY PLANS!
ZIAFCLUF PESTORUM!
ZZAPP
I STILL HAVE OTHER TRICKS AT MY DISPOSAL!

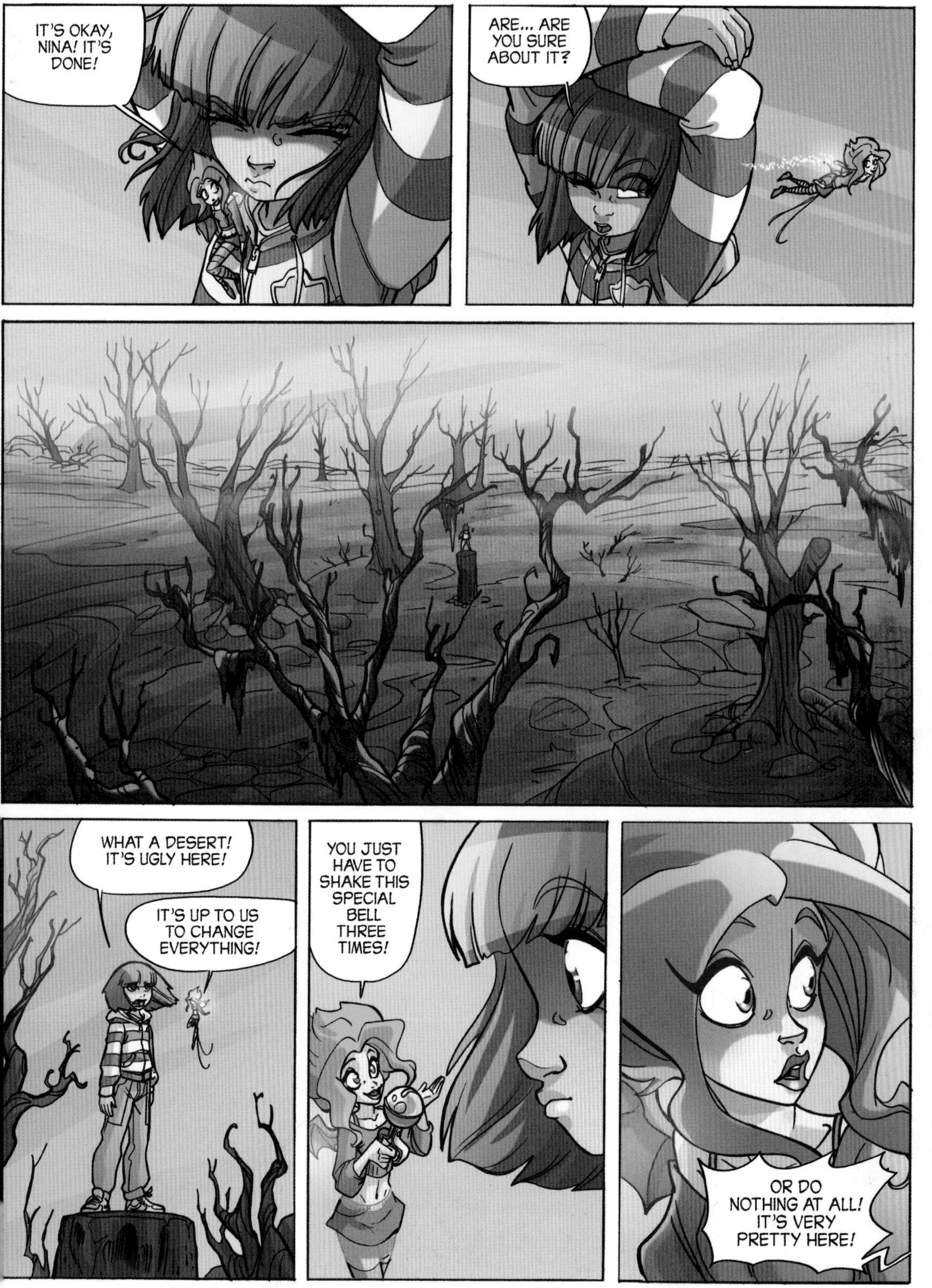

IT'S OKAY, NINA! IT'S DONE!
ARE... ARE YOU SURE ABOUT IT?
WHAT A DESERT! IT'S UGLY HERE!
IT'S UP TO US TO CHANGE EVERYTHING!
YOU JUST HAVE TO SHAKE THIS SPECIAL BELL THREE TIMES!
OR DO NOTHING AT ALL! IT'S VERY PRETTY HERE!

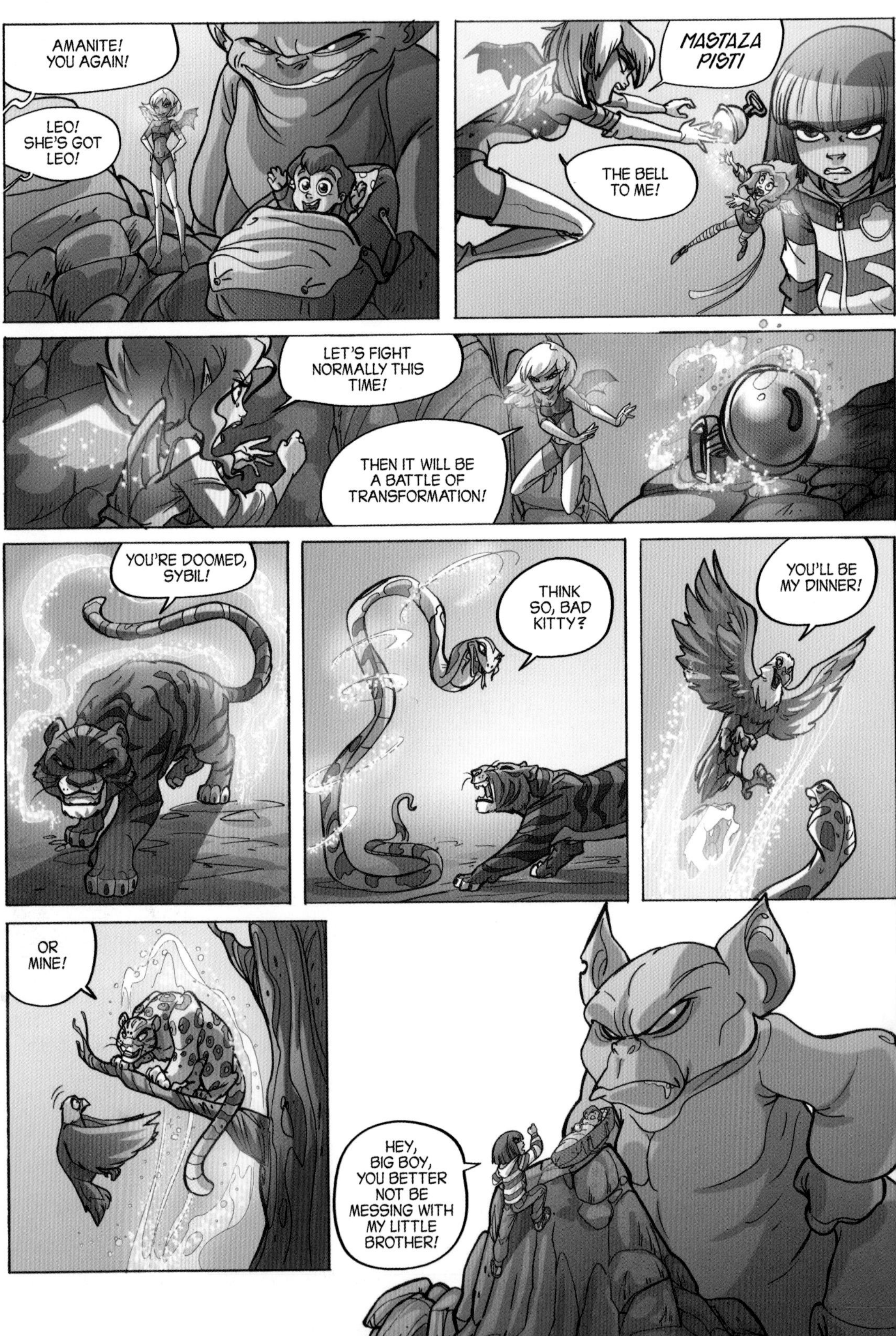
AMANITE! YOU AGAIN!
LEO! SHE'S GOT LEO!
MASTAZA PISTI
THE BELL TO ME!
LET'S FIGHT NORMALLY THIS TIME!
THEN IT WILL BE A BATTLE OF TRANSFORMATION!
YOU'RE DOOMED, SYBIL!
THINK SO, BAD KITTY?
YOU'LL BE MY DINNER!
OR MINE!
HEY, BIG BOY, YOU BETTER NOT BE MESSING WITH MY LITTLE BROTHER!

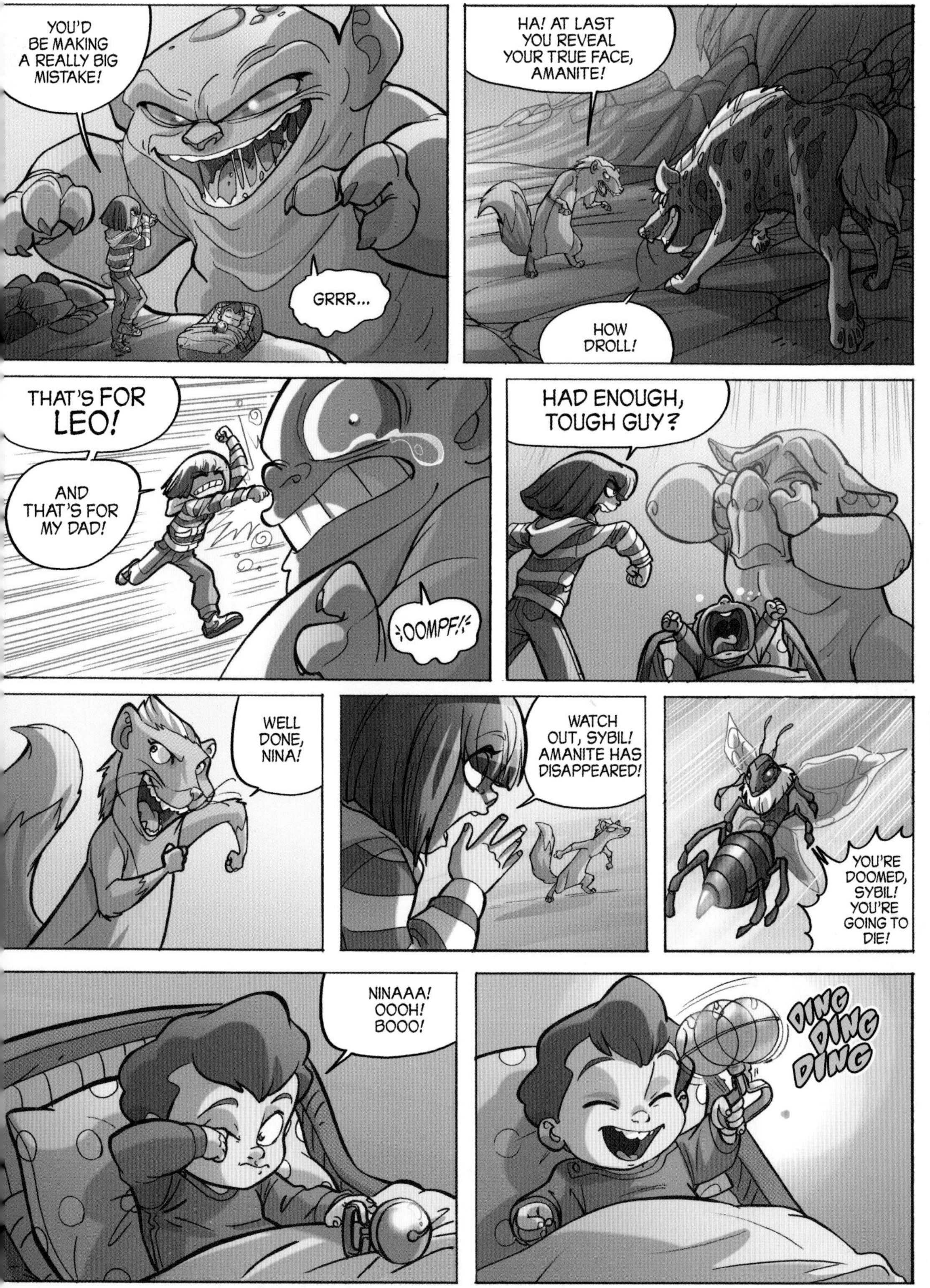
YOU'D BE MAKING A REALLY BIG MISTAKE!
GRRR...
HA! AT LAST YOU REVEAL YOUR TRUE FACE, AMANITE!
HOW DROLL!
THAT'S FOR LEO!
AND THAT'S FOR MY DAD!
OOMPF!
HAD ENOUGH, TOUGH GUY?
WELL DONE, NINA!
WATCH OUT, SYBIL! AMANITE HAS DISAPPEARED!
YOU'RE DOOMED, SYBIL! YOU'RE GOING TO DIE!
NINAAA! OOOH! BOOO!
DING DING DING

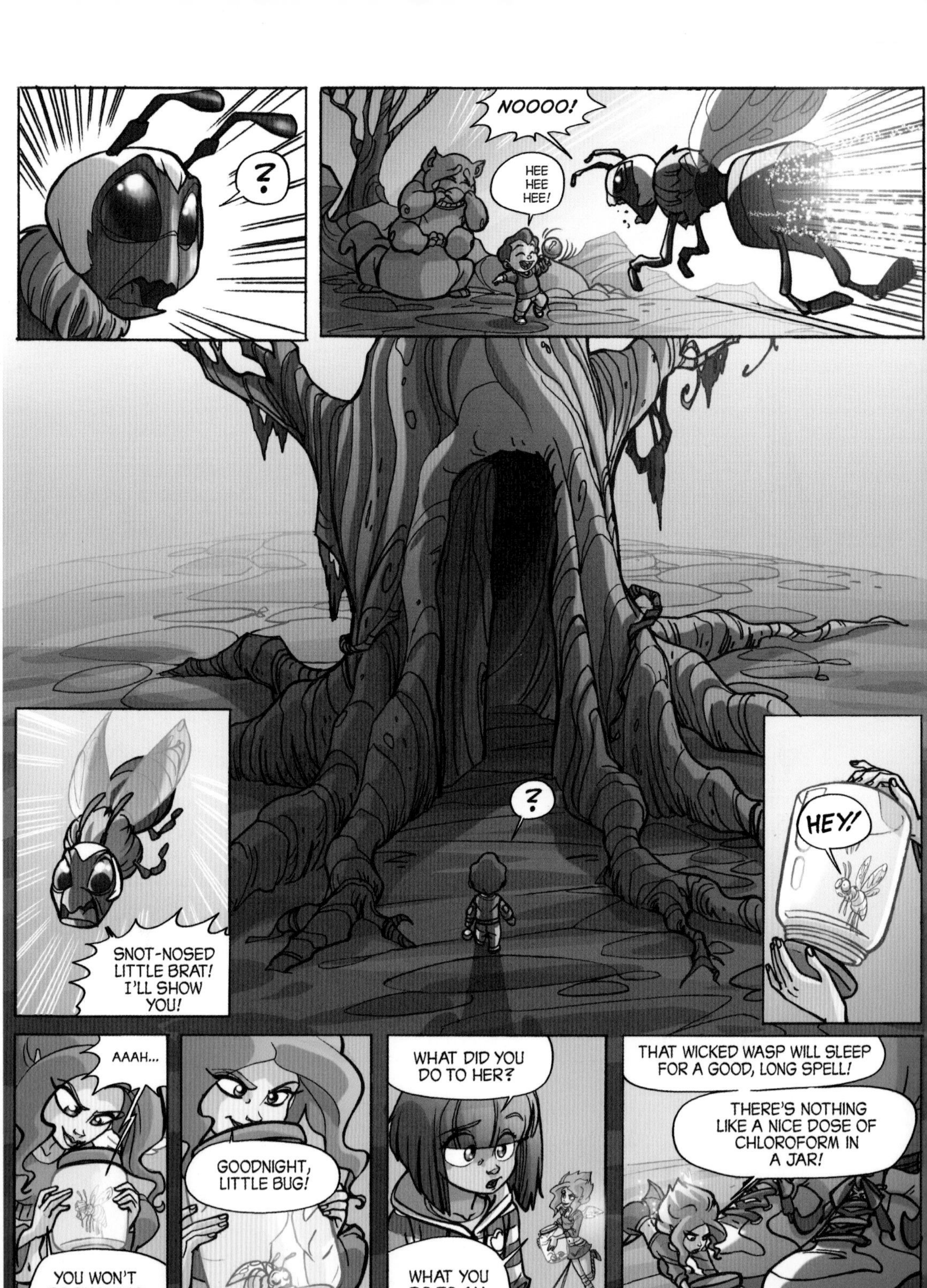
?
NOOOO!
HEE HEE HEE!
SNOT-NOSED LITTLE BRAT! I'LL SHOW YOU!
?
HEY!
AAAH...
YOU WON'T BE SHOWING LEO ANYTHING, YOU PEST!
GOODNIGHT, LITTLE BUG!
WHAT DID YOU DO TO HER?
WHAT YOU DO TO ALL HARMFUL INSECTS...
THAT WICKED WASP WILL SLEEP FOR A GOOD, LONG SPELL!
THERE'S NOTHING LIKE A NICE DOSE OF CHLOROFORM IN A JAR!

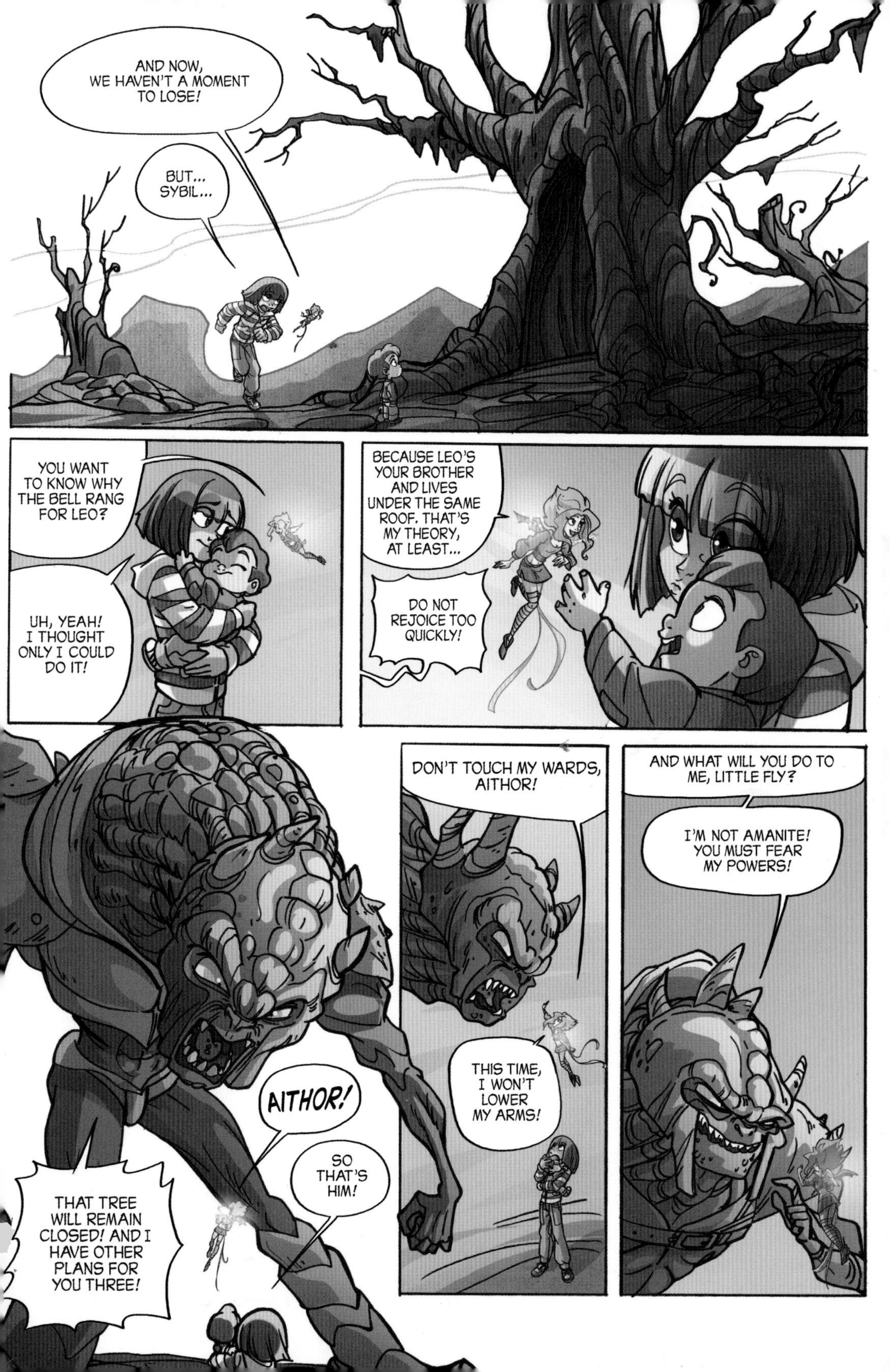
AND NOW, WE HAVEN'T A MOMENT TO LOSE!
BUT... SYBIL...
YOU WANT TO KNOW WHY THE BELL RANG FOR LEO?
UH, YEAH! I THOUGHT ONLY I COULD DO IT!
BECAUSE LEO'S YOUR BROTHER AND LIVES UNDER THE SAME ROOF. THAT'S MY THEORY, AT LEAST...
DO NOT REJOICE TOO QUICKLY!
AITHOR!
SO THAT'S HIM!
THAT TREE WILL REMAIN CLOSED! AND I HAVE OTHER PLANS FOR YOU THREE!
DON'T TOUCH MY WARDS, AITHOR!
THIS TIME, I WON'T LOWER MY ARMS!
AND WHAT WILL YOU DO TO ME, LITTLE FLY?
I'M NOT AMANITE! YOU MUST FEAR MY POWERS!

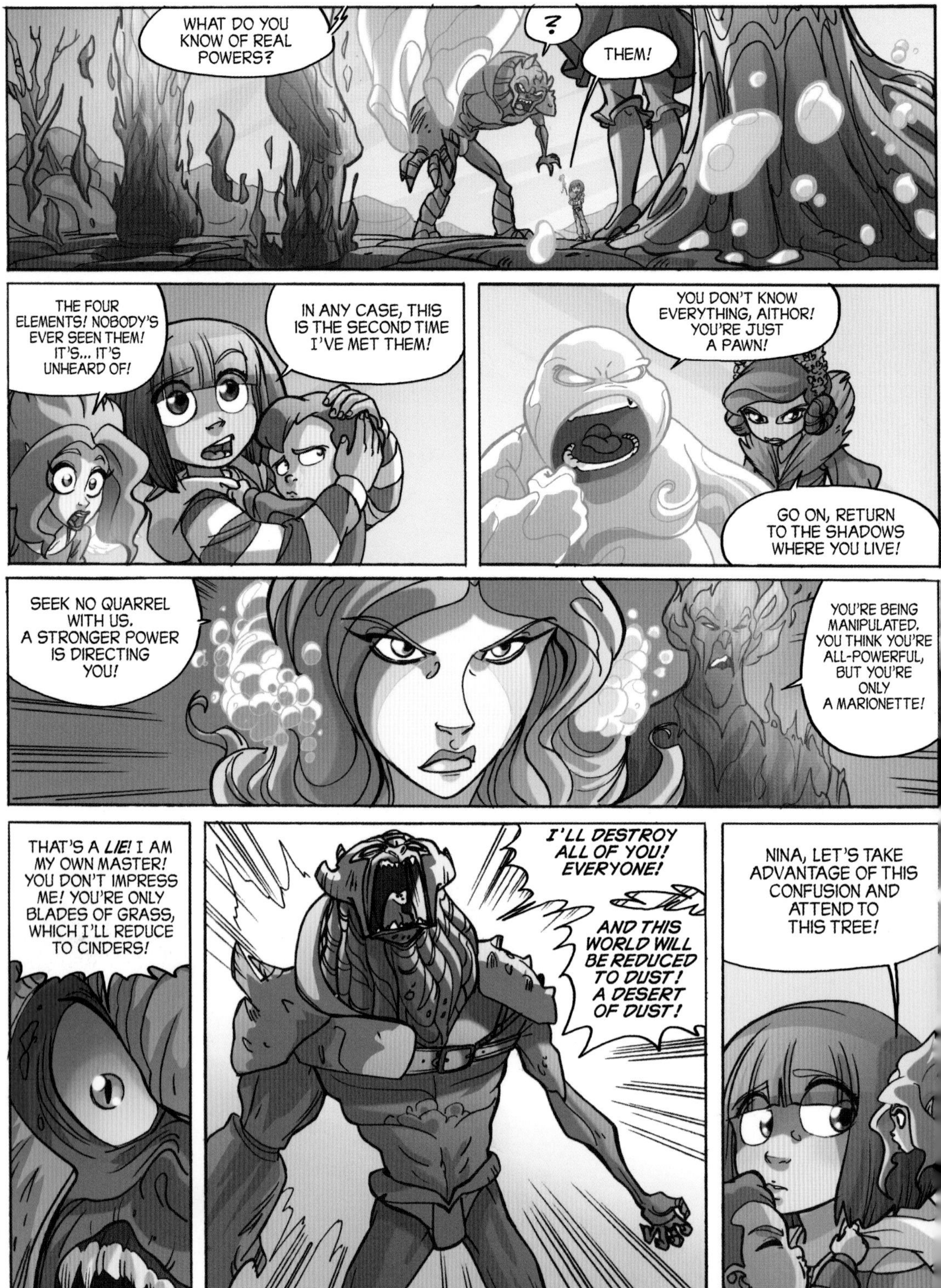
WHAT DO YOU KNOW OF REAL POWERS?
?
THEM!
THE FOUR ELEMENTS! NOBODY'S EVER SEEN THEM! IT'S... IT'S UNHEARD OF!
IN ANY CASE, THIS IS THE SECOND TIME I'VE MET THEM!
YOU DON'T KNOW EVERYTHING, AITHOR! YOU'RE JUST A PAWN!
GO ON, RETURN TO THE SHADOWS WHERE YOU LIVE!
SEEK NO QUARREL WITH US. A STRONGER POWER IS DIRECTING YOU!
YOU'RE BEING MANIPULATED. YOU THINK YOU'RE ALL-POWERFUL, BUT YOU'RE ONLY A MARIONETTE!
THAT'S A *LIE*! I AM MY OWN MASTER! YOU DON'T IMPRESS ME! YOU'RE ONLY BLADES OF GRASS, WHICH I'LL REDUCE TO CINDERS!
I'LL DESTROY ALL OF YOU! EVERYONE!
AND THIS WORLD WILL BE REDUCED TO DUST! A DESERT OF DUST!
NINA, LET'S TAKE ADVANTAGE OF THIS CONFUSION AND ATTEND TO THIS TREE!

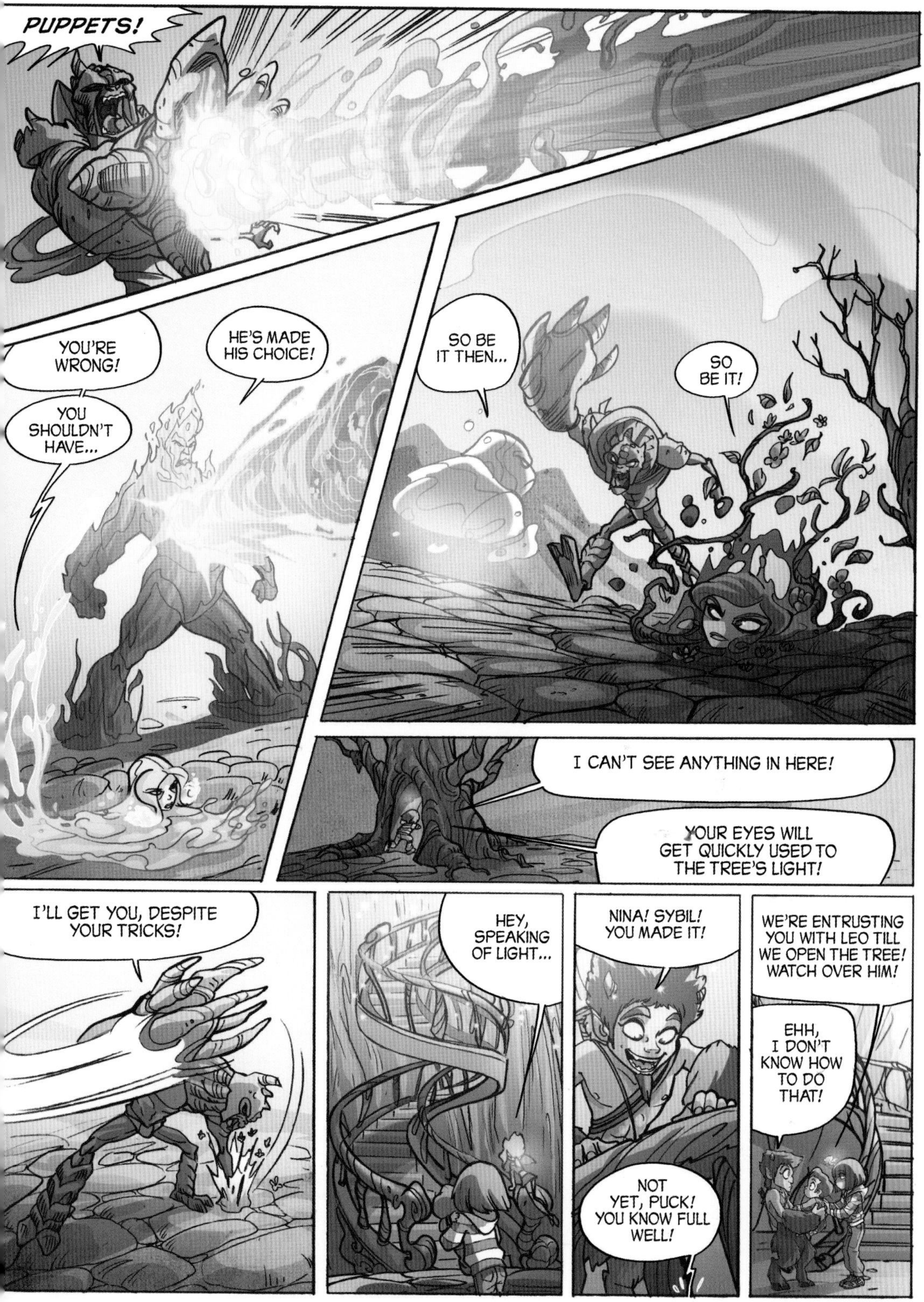
PUPPETS!
YOU'RE WRONG!
YOU SHOULDN'T HAVE...
HE'S MADE HIS CHOICE!
SO BE IT THEN...
SO BE IT!
I CAN'T SEE ANYTHING IN HERE!
YOUR EYES WILL GET QUICKLY USED TO THE TREE'S LIGHT!
I'LL GET YOU, DESPITE YOUR TRICKS!
HEY, SPEAKING OF LIGHT...
NINA! SYBIL! YOU MADE IT!
NOT YET, PUCK! YOU KNOW FULL WELL!
WE'RE ENTRUSTING YOU WITH LEO TILL WE OPEN THE TREE! WATCH OVER HIM!
EHH, I DON'T KNOW HOW TO DO THAT!

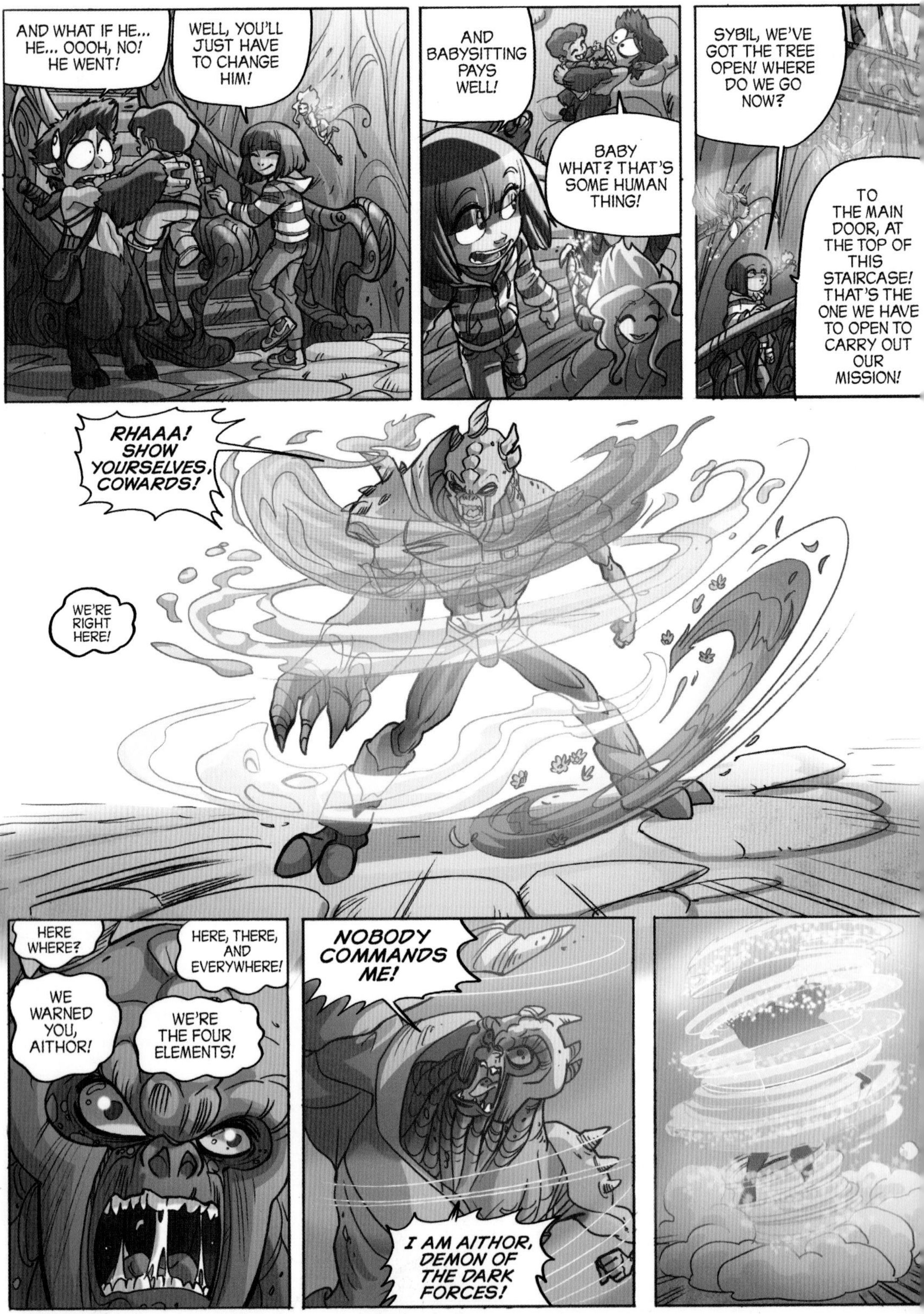
AND WHAT IF HE... HE... OOOH, NO! HE WENT!
WELL, YOU'LL JUST HAVE TO CHANGE HIM!
AND BABYSITTING PAYS WELL!
BABY WHAT? THAT'S SOME HUMAN THING!
SYBIL, WE'VE GOT THE TREE OPEN! WHERE DO WE GO NOW?
TO THE MAIN DOOR, AT THE TOP OF THIS STAIRCASE! THAT'S THE ONE WE HAVE TO OPEN TO CARRY OUT OUR MISSION!
RHAAA! SHOW YOURSELVES, COWARDS!
WE'RE RIGHT HERE!
HERE WHERE?
HERE, THERE, AND EVERYWHERE!
WE WARNED YOU, AITHOR!
WE'RE THE FOUR ELEMENTS!
NOBODY COMMANDS ME!
I AM AITHOR, DEMON OF THE DARK FORCES!

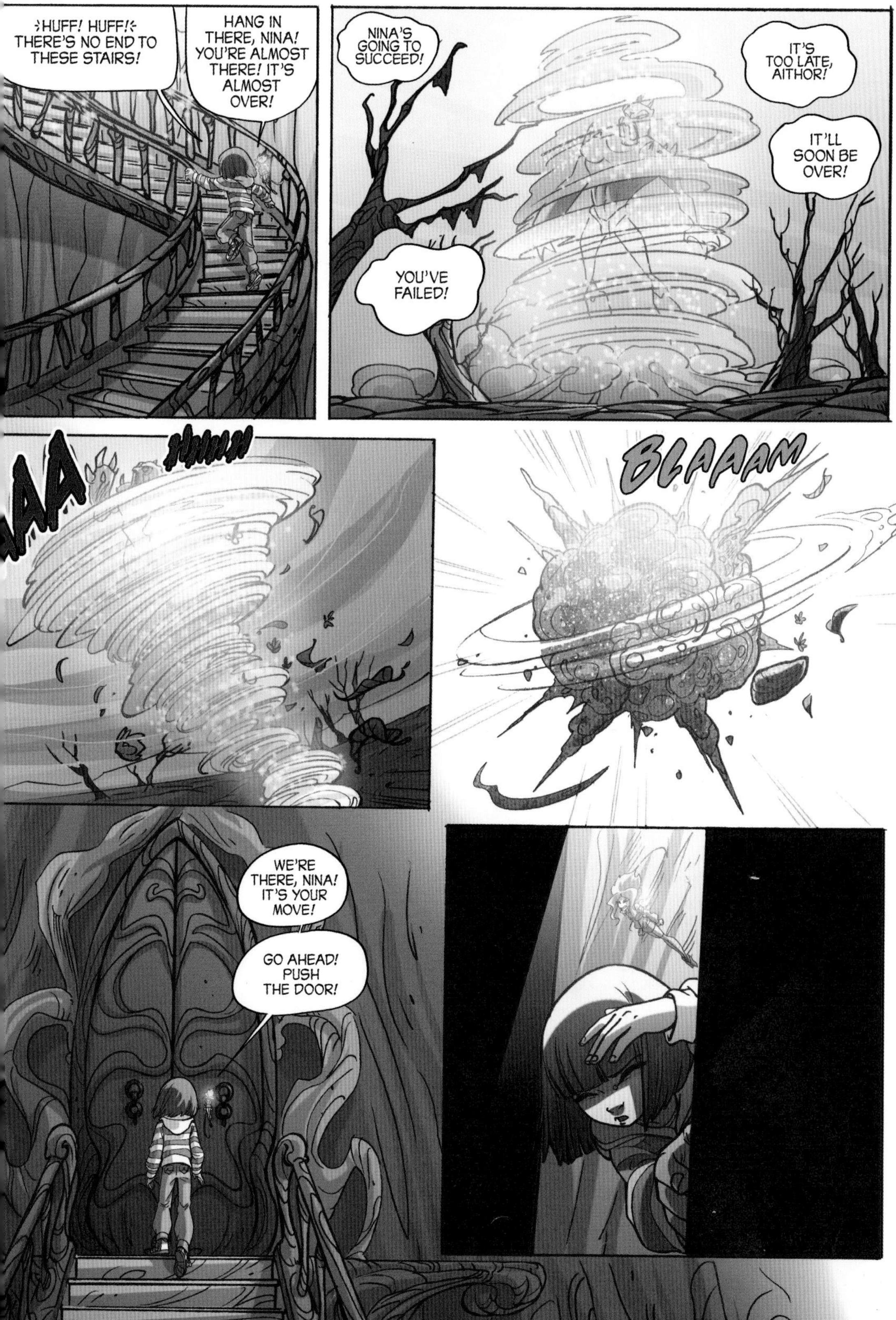

HUFF! HUFF! THERE'S NO END TO THESE STAIRS!
HANG IN THERE, NINA! YOU'RE ALMOST THERE! IT'S ALMOST OVER!
NINA'S GOING TO SUCCEED!
IT'S TOO LATE, AITHOR!
IT'LL SOON BE OVER!
YOU'VE FAILED!
AAA
BLAAAM
WE'RE THERE, NINA! IT'S YOUR MOVE!
GO AHEAD! PUSH THE DOOR!

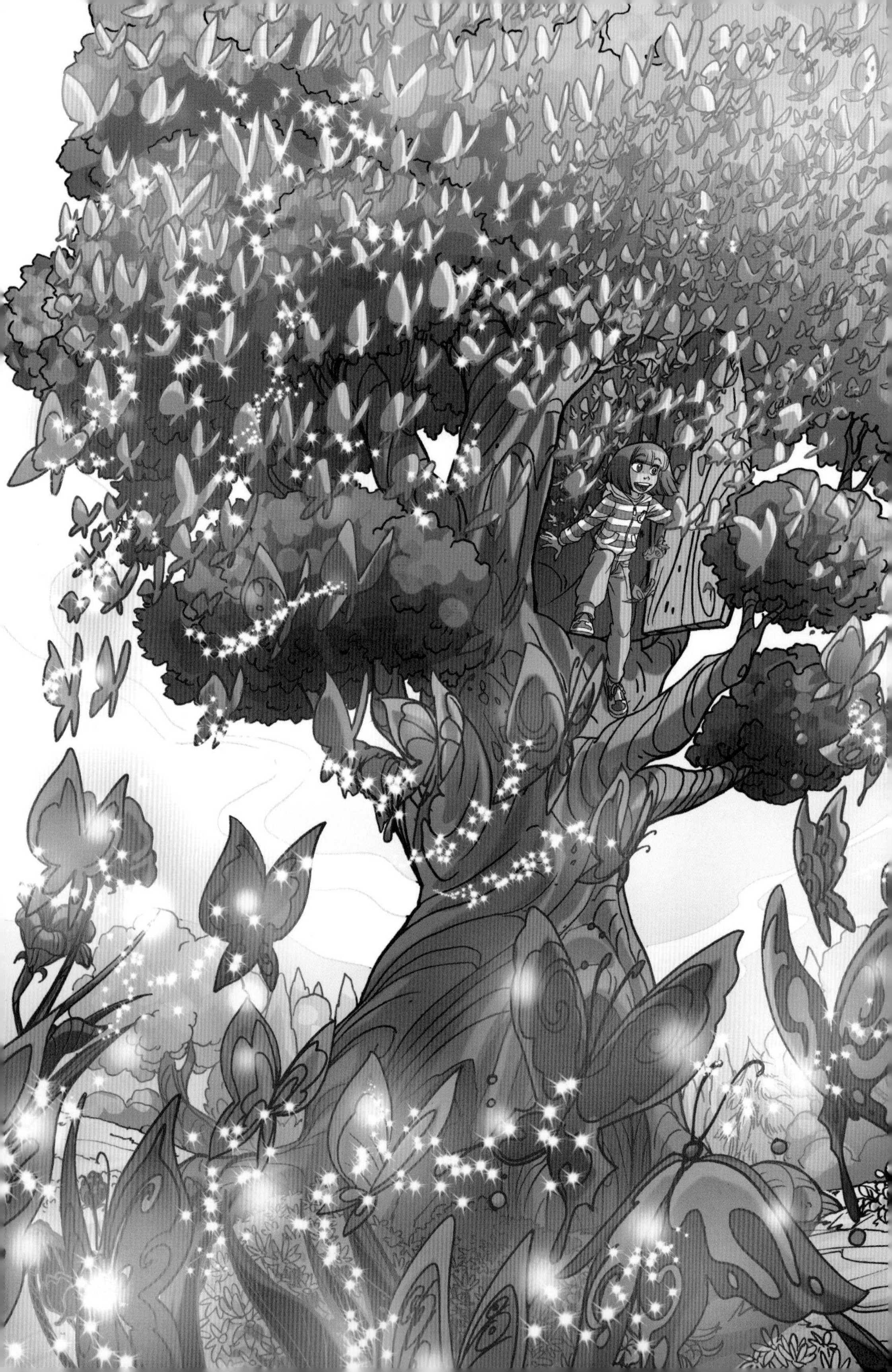

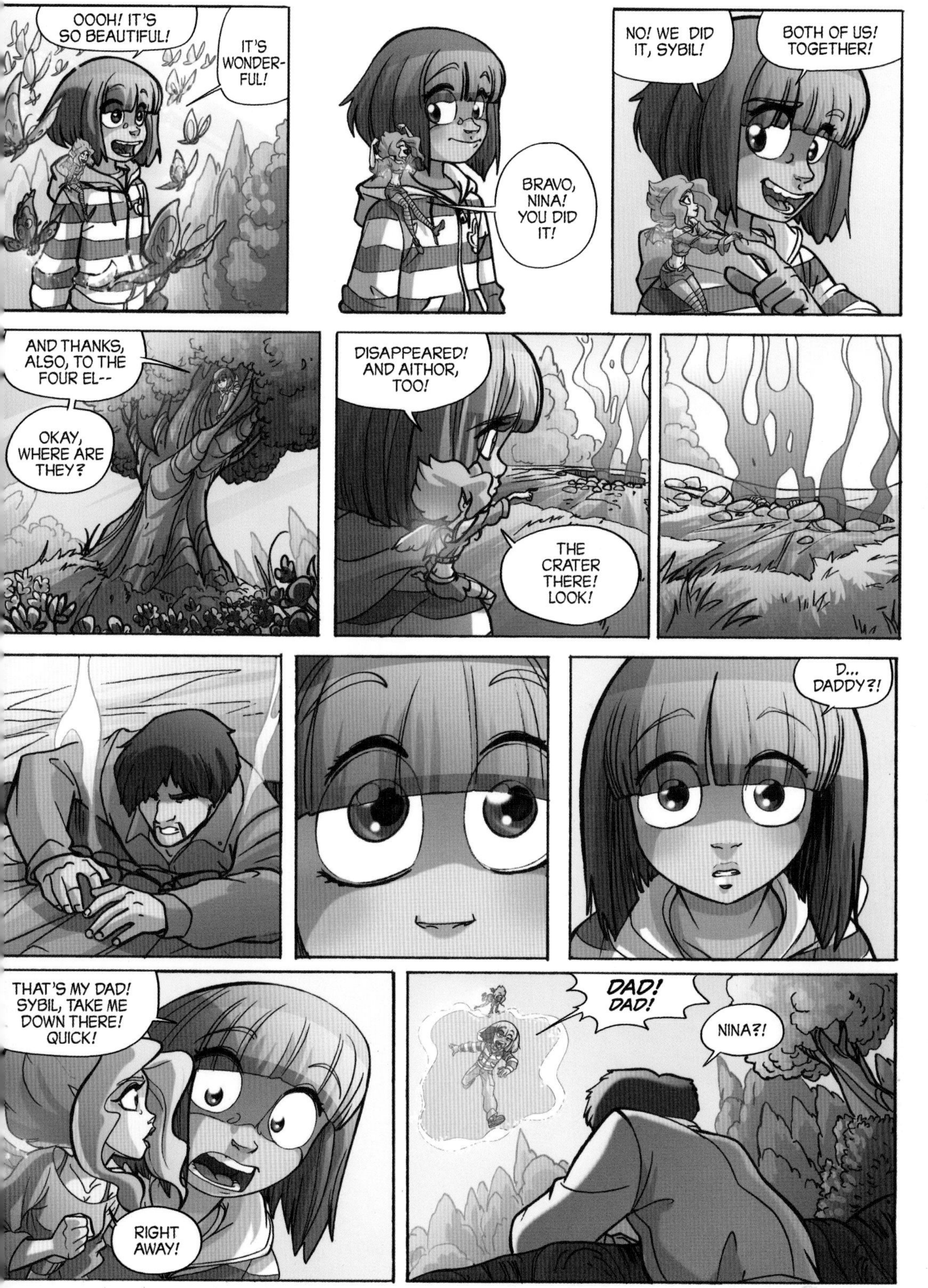

OOOH! IT'S SO BEAUTIFUL!
IT'S WONDERFUL!
BRAVO, NINA! YOU DID IT!
NO! WE DID IT, SYBIL!
BOTH OF US! TOGETHER!
AND THANKS, ALSO, TO THE FOUR EL--
OKAY, WHERE ARE THEY?
DISAPPEARED! AND AITHOR, TOO!
THE CRATER THERE! LOOK!
D... DADDY?!
THAT'S MY DAD! SYBIL, TAKE ME DOWN THERE! QUICK!
RIGHT AWAY!
DAD! DAD!
NINA?!

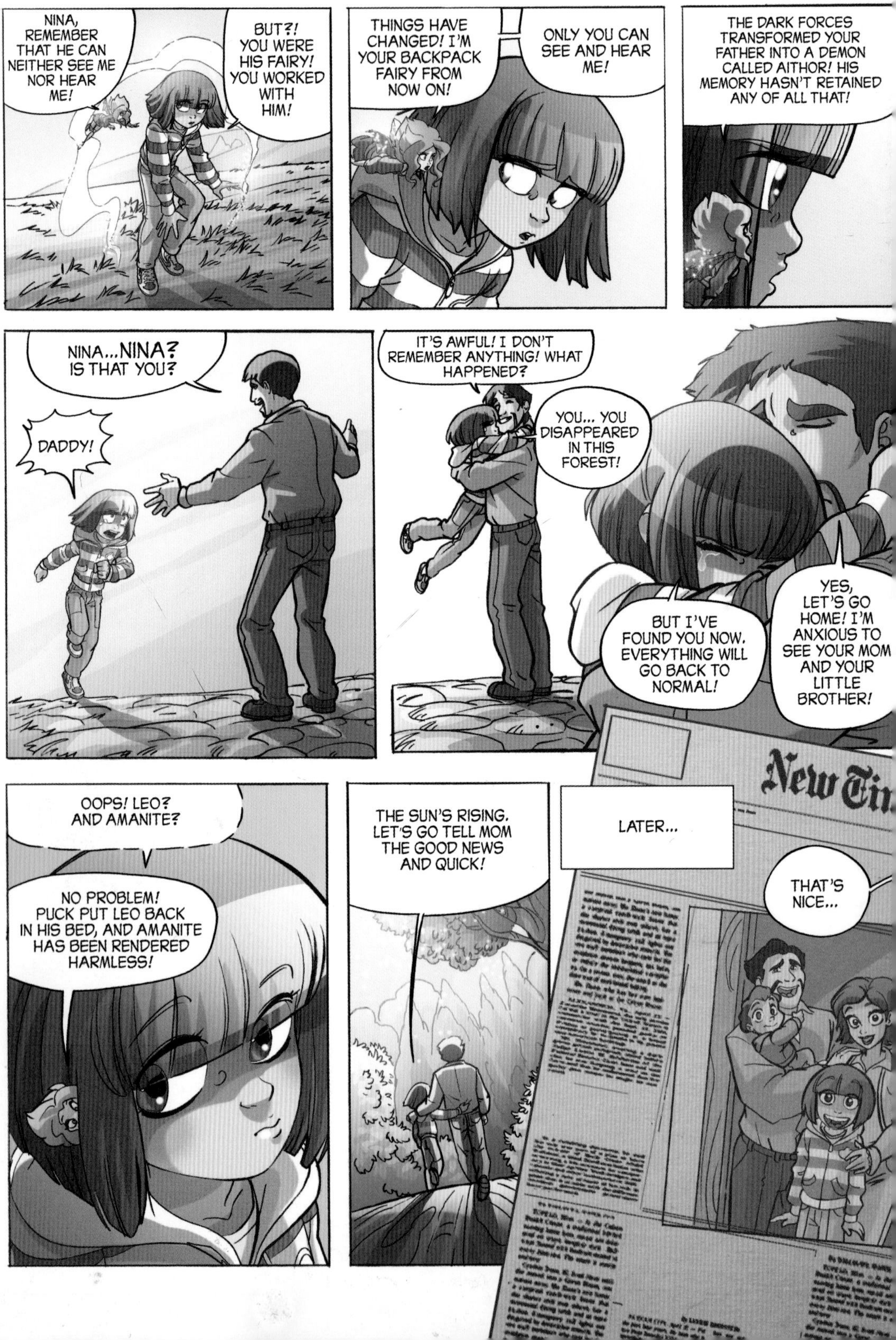
NINA, REMEMBER THAT HE CAN NEITHER SEE ME NOR HEAR ME!
BUT?! YOU WERE HIS FAIRY! YOU WORKED WITH HIM!
THINGS HAVE CHANGED! I'M YOUR BACKPACK FAIRY FROM NOW ON!
ONLY YOU CAN SEE AND HEAR ME!
THE DARK FORCES TRANSFORMED YOUR FATHER INTO A DEMON CALLED AITHOR! HIS MEMORY HASN'T RETAINED ANY OF ALL THAT!
NINA...NINA? IS THAT YOU?
DADDY!
IT'S AWFUL! I DON'T REMEMBER ANYTHING! WHAT HAPPENED?
YOU... YOU DISAPPEARED IN THIS FOREST!
BUT I'VE FOUND YOU NOW. EVERYTHING WILL GO BACK TO NORMAL!
YES, LET'S GO HOME! I'M ANXIOUS TO SEE YOUR MOM AND YOUR LITTLE BROTHER!
OOPS! LEO? AND AMANITE?
NO PROBLEM! PUCK PUT LEO BACK IN HIS BED, AND AMANITE HAS BEEN RENDERED HARMLESS!
THE SUN'S RISING. LET'S GO TELL MOM THE GOOD NEWS AND QUICK!
LATER...
New Ti
THAT'S NICE...

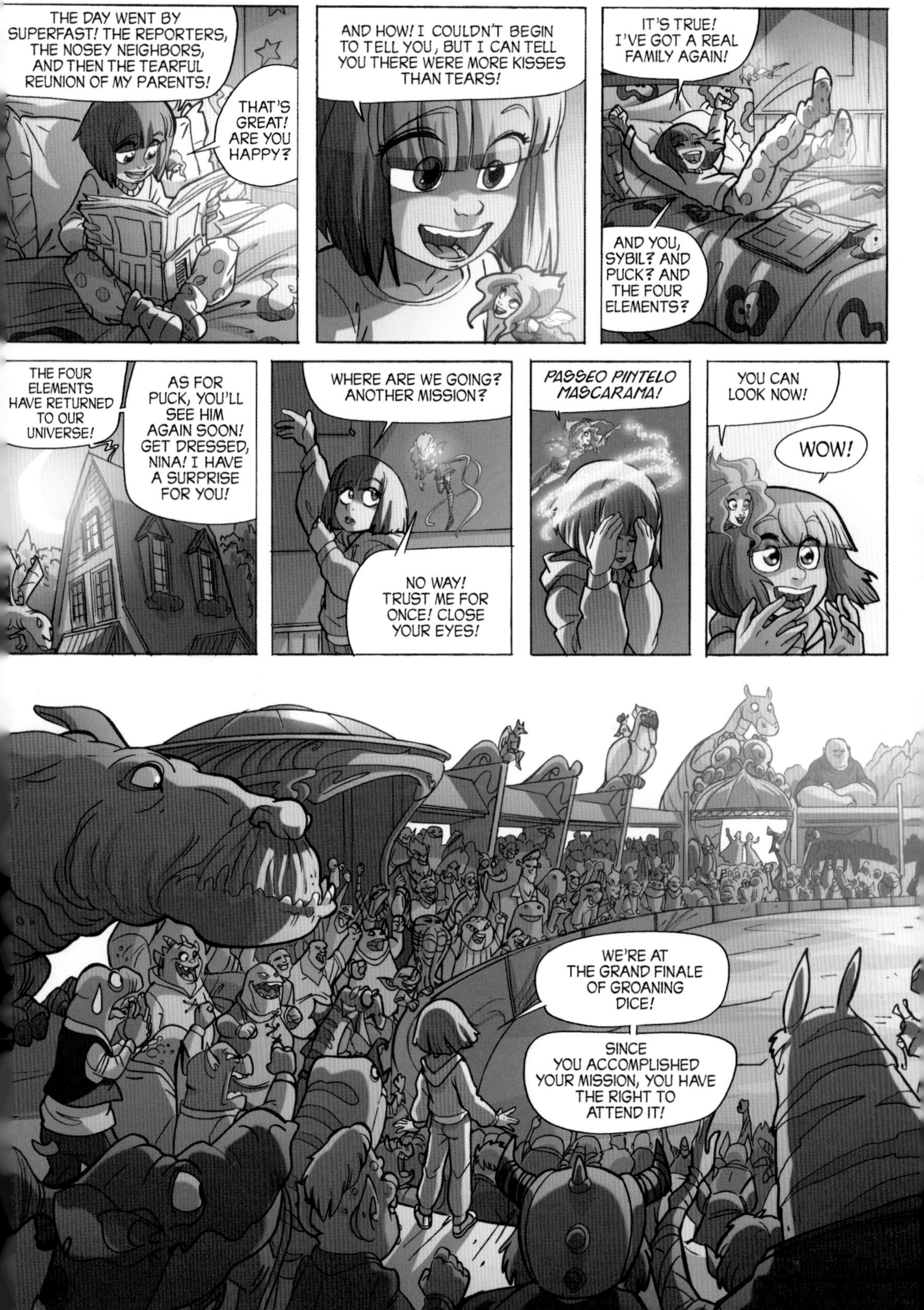

THE DAY WENT BY SUPERFAST! THE REPORTERS, THE NOSEY NEIGHBORS, AND THEN THE TEARFUL REUNION OF MY PARENTS!
THAT'S GREAT! ARE YOU HAPPY?
AND HOW! I COULDN'T BEGIN TO TELL YOU, BUT I CAN TELL YOU THERE WERE MORE KISSES THAN TEARS!
IT'S TRUE! I'VE GOT A REAL FAMILY AGAIN!
AND YOU, SYBIL? AND PUCK? AND THE FOUR ELEMENTS?
THE FOUR ELEMENTS HAVE RETURNED TO OUR UNIVERSE!
AS FOR PUCK, YOU'LL SEE HIM AGAIN SOON! GET DRESSED, NINA! I HAVE A SURPRISE FOR YOU!
WHERE ARE WE GOING? ANOTHER MISSION?
NO WAY! TRUST ME FOR ONCE! CLOSE YOUR EYES!
PASSEO PINTELO MASCARAMA!
YOU CAN LOOK NOW!
WOW!
WE'RE AT THE GRAND FINALE OF GROANING DICE!
SINCE YOU ACCOMPLISHED YOUR MISSION, YOU HAVE THE RIGHT TO ATTEND IT!

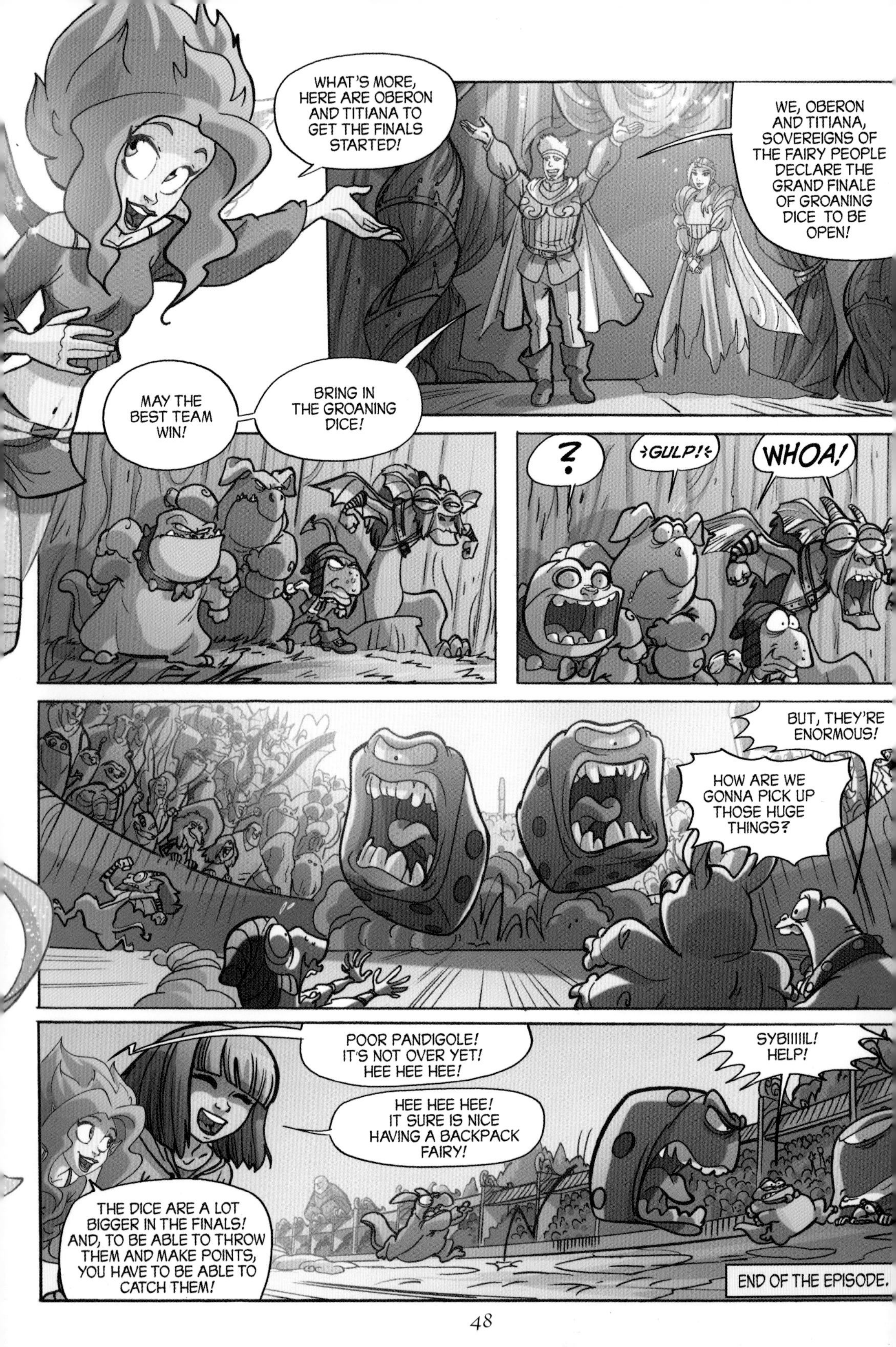
WHAT'S MORE, HERE ARE OBERON AND TITIANA TO GET THE FINALS STARTED!
WE, OBERON AND TITIANA, SOVEREIGNS OF THE FAIRY PEOPLE DECLARE THE GRAND FINALE OF GROANING DICE TO BE OPEN!
MAY THE BEST TEAM WIN!
BRING IN THE GROANING DICE!
?
GULP!
WHOA!
BUT, THEY'RE ENORMOUS!
HOW ARE WE GONNA PICK UP THOSE HUGE THINGS?
POOR PANDIGOLE! IT'S NOT OVER YET! HEE HEE HEE!
HEE HEE HEE! IT SURE IS NICE HAVING A BACKPACK FAIRY!
SYBIIIIIL! HELP!
THE DICE ARE A LOT BIGGER IN THE FINALS! AND, TO BE ABLE TO THROW THEM AND MAKE POINTS, YOU HAVE TO BE ABLE TO CATCH THEM!
END OF THE EPISODE.

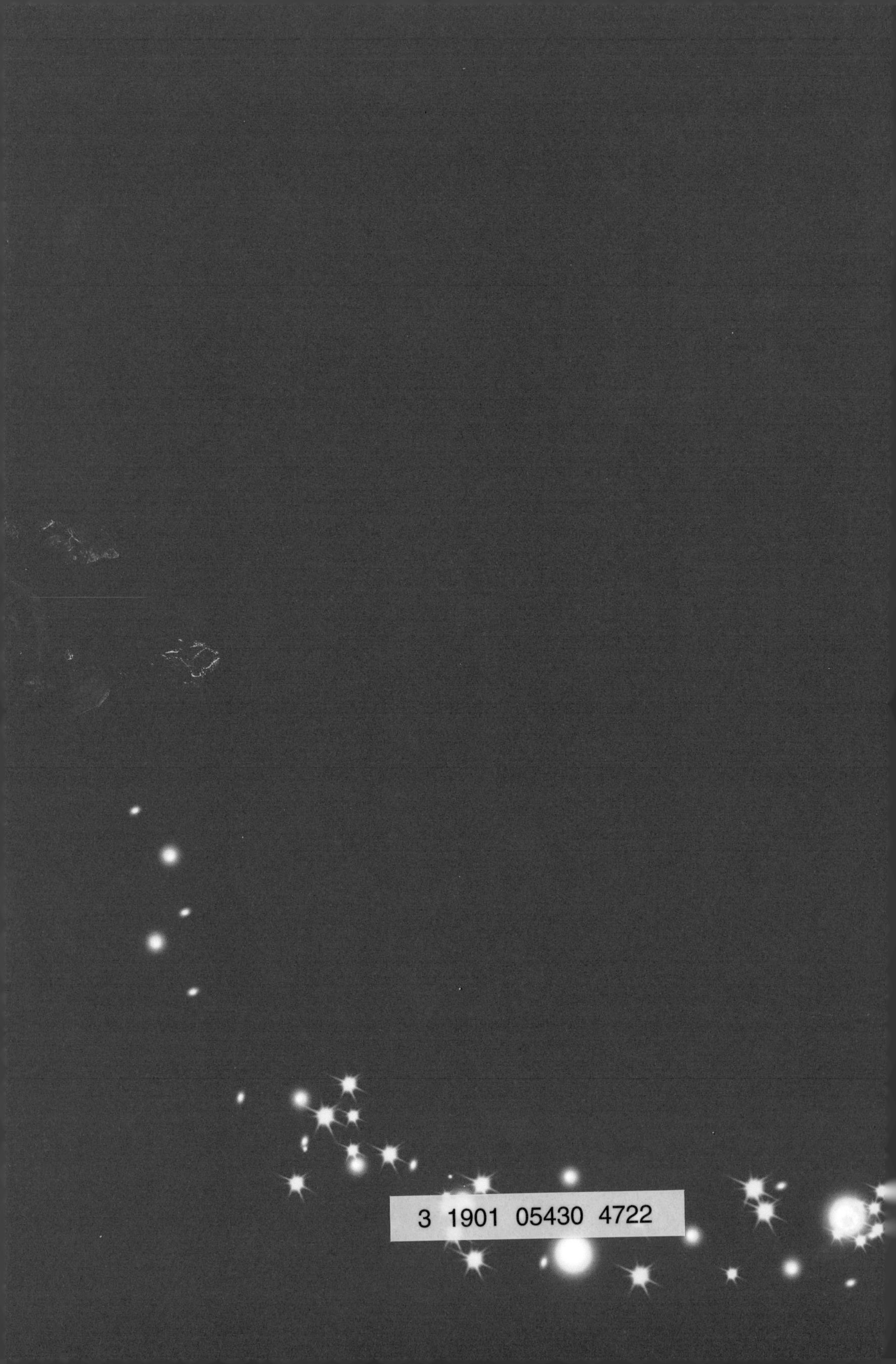